Books, ~

MW01125209

A Heavenly Highland Inn Cozy Mystery

Cindy Bell

Copyright © 2014 Cindy Bell

All rights reserved.

This is a work of fiction. The characters, incidents and locations portrayed in this book and the names herein are fictitious. Any similarity to or identification with the locations, names, characters or history of any person, product or entity is entirely coincidental and unintentional.

All trademarks and brands referred to in this book are for illustrative purposes only, are the property of their respective owners and not affiliated with this publication in any way. Any trademarks are being used without permission, and the publication of the trademark is not authorized by, associated with or sponsored by the trademark owner.

ISBN-13: 978-1501051418

ISBN-10: 1501051415

More Cozy Mysteries by Cindy Bell

Dune House Cozy Mystery Series

Seaside Secrets

Boats and Bad Guys

Heavenly Highland Inn Cozy Mystery Series

Murdering the Roses

Dead in the Daisies

Killing the Carnations

Drowning the Daffodils

Suffocating the Sunflowers

Books, Bullets and Blooms

Table of Contents

Chapter One

Vicky had the distinct impression that her Aunt Ida was up to something. At the Heavenly Highland Inn where she and her aunt both lived, it was hard not to be aware of everything that was happening in each other's lives. Vicky and her older sister, Sarah, owned and ran the inn together, ever since their parents had tragically passed away. Sarah lived with her husband and her two children not far from the inn, so she didn't always get to witness her aunt's antics.

Aunt Ida was a very rambunctious soul. She had traveled the world, could speak several languages, and was well trained in martial arts. She was not the typical motherly type but she did keep a close eye on her nieces, who in turn did their best to keep a close eye on her. So, when Vicky couldn't find her aunt in her room, or in Vicky's apartment in the inn, or in the beautifully manicured gardens behind the inn, or in the kitchen where she would usually be harassing Chef Henry for a sample of his latest dish, Vicky was a little concerned. Although, she had been seeing less of her aunt lately, ever since she had begun dating Rex, a biker who was completely smitten with Aunt Ida, a missing Aunt Ida was a dangerous Aunt Ida.

Aunt Ida was closing in on her seventies, but she was always dressed in outlandish fashions, the brighter the better, and kept her short hair stylish in whatever color she chose to dye it. She could have easily passed for being in her forties, but she flirted like she was still in her twenties. Vicky, on the other hand was decidedly understated compared to her aunt. She was always wearing a suit or a smart dress while working and would dress in jeans or casual slacks and whatever top was comfortable, when she wasn't working. She kept her dark brown hair brushed and cleaned but that was about it. The most remarkable thing about her was her deep green eyes which always gave away her emotions, and prevented her from being able to tell a good lie. She adored her aunt, and admired the free-spirit that she was. But, she was still a little concerned about what she might be up to.

***

Giggling and shrieking filtered out into the hallway beside the small restaurant nestled inside the lobby of the Heavenly Highland Inn. Vicky paused beside the glass door and peered inside. Aunt Ida was holed up in the restaurant with her Murder Mystery Book Club. They usually met on Thursday nights, so since it was Tuesday morning, this was unusual to begin with. But then anything that particular group did, was a little bit unusual. Their trivia games consisted of serial killers and deadly poisons. It was a little unsettling.

The group, gathered around one of the large tables inside the restaurant, was an assorted bunch with a few women Ida's age, and a handful of younger members. There were two men in the group, who were giggling just as loudly as their female counterparts.

"Do you think it's safe to go in?" Sarah asked nervously as she stepped up beside Vicky. Vicky glanced over at her older sister and cringed.

"I don't know," she shook her head. "What I don't understand is what could be so funny about a murder mystery?" she tilted her head to the side.

"Oh, you haven't heard?" Sarah asked and pushed back her wavy, blonde hair with a gleeful smile. It wasn't often that she knew about something before her younger sister did, since Vicky was dating a police officer she always had the dirt first. "They're all in a tizzy because Aunt Ida's letter writing campaign has finally paid off."

"What letter writing campaign?" Vicky asked with confusion.

"Well, you know they love reading that one author, Preston Price?" Sarah reminded her.

"Yes, I remember her mentioning him," Vicky nodded as she ducked away from the door before she could be spotted.

"Well, it turns out he is launching his next book and was looking for a place to hold his launch. Aunt Ida got it into her head that if she and the rest of her book club wrote enough letters he would decide to use the inn. And it turns out, he did," Sarah laughed and shook her head. "Aunt Ida can do anything she puts her mind to," she said with admiration.

"That's for sure," Vicky agreed with a grin. "Well, I guess we have a book launch to plan."

"I already have this weekend cleared out to accommodate him," Sarah explained. "We didn't have much planned so it wasn't too hard."

"It's a little last minute isn't it?" Vicky asked with surprise.

"He insisted it had to be this weekend," Sarah shrugged. "I figured you could throw together an after-party."

"Sure," Vicky nodded. While Sarah was more in charge of running the inn and booking guests, Vicky was the event planner. "Maybe I'll give it a morgue theme," she giggled.

"Ugh," Sarah shuddered. "Can you imagine?" she shook her head.

As Vicky turned back towards the restaurant, the door swung open and Aunt Ida burst forth in all of her pastel-splashed glory.

"I'm so excited," Ida said happily as she hugged Sarah and then Vicky. "It's like having a celebrity at the inn!"

Vicky was thrilled to see her aunt so excited. "Don't worry we'll make sure everything is perfect," she assured her aunt.

"Oh, I know it will be," Ida said breathlessly. She clasped her hands together beneath her chin and sighed dreamily. "To think, by this time Saturday I'll be looking into the eyes of Preston Price."

"Oh, Aunt Ida," Sarah laughed with disbelief. Vicky cast a smile in Sarah's direction.

"Well, it isn't just any man that can keep Aunt Ida's attention for hours. You love being taken into another world when you read his books, don't you Aunt Ida?" Vicky asked her aunt with a wink.

"Exactly!" Ida said with a grin.

"Well, I better get started on the party planning," Vicky said as she hugged her aunt again.

***

As Vicky was walking back towards her apartment, which took up a large portion of the main floor of the inn, her cell phone began ringing. She pulled it out of her pocket to see that it was her boyfriend, Mitchell. They had been dating for quite some time but she still felt a little thrill every time she saw his name on the caller ID.

"Hello?" she said as she unlocked the door to her apartment.

"I just needed to hear your voice," Mitchell sighed into the phone. Vicky smiled as she closed the door behind her. It was Mitchell's voice that she loved hearing, mainly because of his southern accent that made all his words sound as smooth and sweet as honey.

"Aw, having a bad day?" she asked as she dropped down onto the couch in her living room.

"Not really, just missing you," Mitchell replied with a hint of sadness in his voice. Mitchell had been having an unspoken war with his boss, Sheriff McDonnell. Sheriff McDonnell seemed to have a love, hate relationship with Mitchell. At the moment it was hate as he seemed to feel that Mitchell was a bit of a loose cannon and bent the rules on a few too many occasions, most of those occasions had been for Vicky's sake.

As a result he had been finding every excuse he could to pile on the overtime for Mitchell. Mitchell, who could have easily complained and had the Sheriff disciplined for his obvious abuse of power, had been just as stubborn by acting as if the overtime didn't bother him at all. It was really an amusing battle, except for the fact that it meant Vicky and Mitchell didn't get a lot of time to be alone together.

"I'm sorry, honey," Vicky murmured into the phone as she stretched out along the couch. "Want me to drop by with some donuts?" she suggested.

"Not all cops eat donuts," he pointed out with mock offense.

"But Sheriff McDonnell does, and if I buy him an entire dozen he'll be stuck in his office for a while. Do you still have a key to the supply closet?" Vicky inquired innocently.

"Vicky!" Mitchell laughed.

"What?" Vicky inquired with a smile. "Desperate times call for desperate measures!"

"I don't want to hide in a closet with you," Mitchell replied impatiently. "I want to wake up next to you."

"Well, then come spend the night," Vicky invited. "Or maybe I could curl up under your desk?"

"I can't, I'm covering the night shift," Mitchell sighed. "But that under the desk thing might work out," he added with a smile in his voice.

"Unfortunately, I have a last minute book launch and party to plan," Vicky frowned as she sat up on the couch again. Mitchell was being playful but she knew how much it bothered him not to be with her more often. While Vicky was more accustomed to being alone, Mitchell seemed to want to spend every minute he could with her. She had to admit that lately she had been longing to wake up and look right into his eyes.

"I guess we'll see each other sometime this weekend then," he sighed into the phone.

"You should come to the book launch," Vicky suggested. "It's for a crime writer, maybe you could give him some tips."

"Sure, about how to file paperwork and be a friendly crossing guard," Mitchell laughed at the idea.

"Are you complaining about the lack of crime, Mitchell?" Vicky grinned.

"Not exactly," he replied and sighed again. "I'll be there," he promised. "Don't work too hard."

"I'd say the same to you but I don't think you'll listen," Vicky countered.

"He's going to break eventually," Mitchell said with confidence. "I've been killing him with kindness."

"Hmm, sounds like a new crime novel," Vicky laughed.

"I'll discuss it with the writer," Mitchell replied lightheartedly. "See you soon, sweetheart."

"Not soon enough," Vicky replied and blew a kiss into the phone. As she hung up she frowned.

Things had been a little spotty between the two of them when they first started dating, with Vicky being a little too inquisitive for her own good when it came to police work and being cautious about committing to a relationship. But eventually Mitchell had adjusted to the idea that Vicky just happened to land in the middle of most things and he was happy to take things slow. Still, she wished they had the chance to just spend some solid time together away from their jobs.

Chapter Two

Over the next few days Vicky spent almost all of her time on the party plans. Since it was important to her aunt, it was extremely important to her. She was heading to the kitchen to check on Chef Henry's supply of champagne when she heard a squeal from the lobby. She smiled to herself as she was certain this meant that Preston Price had arrived. As she walked back towards the lobby she saw Aunt Ida in her sexiest dress. Vicky had to hide a smile as she watched her aunt fawn over Preston who was finishing things up with Sarah at the front desk.

"Oh, do let me show you around," Ida pleaded as she draped her arm over him. "I think you'll love this place. Maybe you could even use it in your next murder mystery. Wouldn't that be great publicity, Vicky?" she said happily as Vicky walked up to the desk.

Vicky smiled and nodded. She thought that the inn had had more than its fair share of real murder mysteries, but Ida was so pleased with her idea she didn't point it out. It was wonderful to see her so excited.

"Hello, Mr. Price," Vicky said, the name sounded a bit strange once she said it.

"Please, call me Preston," Preston replied as he smiled tolerantly at Ida and nodded a greeting to Vicky. "I appreciate you putting this all together so quickly for me."

"Of course," Vicky nodded. "I arranged for the special informal meeting between you and the book club this afternoon. I hope that will work for you?"

"Sounds great," he smiled brightly. "Without Ida and her friends I never would have known about this gem of an inn."

"Well, we're happy to have you," Sarah said smoothly.

"We have some time before the meeting," Ida smiled. "I'd love to show you the gardens."

"I'd enjoy that," Preston nodded and walked off with Ida hanging on his arm. Vicky leaned against the desk and watched them walk away. Preston seemed nice enough. He was wearing a simple suit, his blondish hair was trimmed in a classic cut, and his expression was kind. But he also seemed a little nervous.

"Looks like Rex has some competition," Sarah giggled as she watched her aunt lead Preston away.

"Hmm," Vicky said as she pointed to the back of the book that Preston had left on the desk. "It says here he's married."

"Oops, she better mind her manners," Sarah laughed again. "Do you have everything you need for the party?"

"Everything is coming together fine," Vicky assured her before heading back off to the kitchen.

***

Mitchell arrived at the inn just in time for the meeting with the book club. He looked a little harried from lack of sleep, but that didn't diminish the impact of his handsome presence for Vicky. She threw herself into his arms the moment he walked through the door.

"Assaulting a police officer?" he asked with surprise and a smile before kissing her softly.

"Well, if I have to abduct you, I'm willing to do the time," Vicky replied playfully.

"I'm not going to turn in," he grinned and kissed her again.

"I wish we could skip the meeting, but I know Aunt Ida will be disappointed if I'm not there," Vicky sighed. "This event is very important to her."

"Then, let's not be late," Mitchell suggested. "Who knows when Sheriff McDonnell is going to notice I'm missing."

"That man..." Vicky began to say.

"He's going to be my boss for a long time, Vicky," Mitchell reminded her. "I've got to earn my way into his good graces somehow."

"I know, I know," Vicky griped before leading him into the restaurant. Vicky had arranged the tables and chairs so they were facing a table in the front of the restaurant. Preston was seated there, and the members of the book club had arranged themselves at the tables across from him. Of course Ida was front and center.

"Well, I know that it's not me that any of you are interested in," Preston laughed a little as he sat back in his chair. "So, I'd like to find out what you thought about the book, and whether you have any questions."

One of the men in the group raised his hand quickly. Everyone looked at him expectantly.

"Yes, you had a question?" Preston asked.

"I do," he said firmly. "My name is Brandon Derger, maybe you've read my emails," he said calmly.

"Oh, you're Brandon," Preston replied uncomfortably. "Yes, I've received your numerous emails."

"Good, then you should know that I am a huge fan of your books," Brandon said in a serious tone.

"I know that you like correcting any errors in my writing," Preston offered a tight smile.

"You're welcome," Brandon smiled for the first time.

"Your question, Brandon?" Preston asked and shifted in his chair.

"It's not so much a question, as it is an observation," Brandon explained. "In this new book the body of the victim is found slumped over the bar," Brandon pointed out as he pushed his wire-rimmed glasses back up along his nose. "However, the medical examiner then finds that the victim has been dead for several hours. Since it does take some time for rigor mortis to set in, I just can't understand how his body would have stayed in that position. Shouldn't he have slid off the edge of the bar, and ended up on the floor? Are you really comfortable with that kind of misleading representation of the dying process in your book?" His gray eyes searched Preston's as he studied him intently.

"Ah Brandon, what a loyal fan you are," Preston said with a wide smile. "It seems to me that you have all the details right. However, you might have overlooked one small thing."

"What's that?" Brandon asked with confusion.

"The victim was grasping the inside edge of the bar when he was shot from behind. His hand would have clasped even tighter when the bullet struck his body, so his fingers obviously became wedged between the rail and the edge of the bar, causing his body to remain in the same position until he was found," Preston explained confidently.

Vicky overheard Aunt Ida whispering to the lady next to her. "Isn't he an amazing writer?" she giggled. "He thinks of everything!"

Vicky stared at Preston, something about him left her intrigued. It was hard for her to imagine someone thinking out the tiniest details of a death so clearly.

"I don't think he's going to need any tips from me," Mitchell said as he leaned close to her ear, his deep southern drawl lingered in Vicky's ears like the sweetest song.

"Mitchell," she smiled up at him as he rested a hand lightly on her shoulder. "I'm sure there's plenty he could still learn from you."

Ida spotted Mitchell and Vicky. She waved and silently slipped out of her chair to walk over to them.

"Mitchell, I'm so glad you're here, I didn't think you would be able to make it," Ida said with a warm smile.

"Of course, I just had to shake off Sheriff McDonnell, he's still piling on the overtime," he rolled his eyes at that.

"Well, he should be," Ida said sternly.

Both Vicky and Mitchell looked over at her with surprise. "Why do you say that, Aunt Ida?" Vicky asked. "You know Mitchell didn't do anything wrong to deserve such treatment."

"No, he did everything right," Ida agreed as she smiled fondly at Mitchell. "After all you are the best officer in our little town, and we all feel safer when you are on patrol." Vicky was relieved that Aunt Ida had finally forgiven Mitchell for giving her a speeding ticket.

"Aw," Vicky grinned at her aunt and winked at Mitchell.

"That is very kind of you," Mitchell smiled warmly at Ida. "But there are many other well-trained officers. Honestly, I'm looking forward to having a day or two off so I can spend some real time with Vicky. Wouldn't that be nice?" he asked as he looked down at her.

"It would be," Vicky agreed as she reached up to softly grasp his hand which still lingered on her shoulder.

"Shh listen," Ida said as she turned her attention back to Preston. "He might reveal another twist."

"Is there going to be another book added to the series?" Pamela asked hopefully. "I've been hoping maybe there would be a twist where the death was faked, anything to keep such a great story going."

"I'm sorry, at this time, I don't intend to write anything further in this series," Preston said with a slight frown. A few groans of disappointment filled the room. "But perhaps I'll start on something new," he suggested and smiled at the small group gathered around him. He was very charismatic which was something that Vicky hadn't expected from a writer. She had always pictured writers as being aloof and living in their own little world to some degree. She was just a little envious of that aspect.

"I have some ideas, if you'd like to hear them," Brandon suggested eagerly. "In fact I was thinking that you could bring one of the supporting characters, like Jake, to the forefront and let him have a spin-off."

Preston cleared his throat and sat back in his chair. "I appreciate the input, Brandon, and you have some great ideas. Maybe you should start writing stories of your own?" he suggested.

"I can't," Brandon frowned. "I've tried. But they're just words on paper."

"Well, Brandon, you know that there are a lot of great writers out there, maybe you could find a new series to follow," Preston suggested. "In the meantime please feel free to read over some of my past works."

"But what about my ideas?" Brandon pressed, drawing some uncomfortable glances from the people around him.

"As I said, I won't be continuing this series," Preston said more firmly. "Jake is not a strong enough character for a spin-off."

"What?" Brandon said with disbelief and stood up from his chair. "That's nuts. Jake is a very strong character. He was much more interesting..."

"Brandon, calm down," Preston requested sternly.

Vicky felt Mitchell's hand pull away from her shoulder and come to rest on the butt of his weapon as he took his police officer stance. The friendly meeting was quickly taking a darker turn.

"I'm not going to calm down!" Brandon nearly shouted. "First you kill off the main character, then you talk down about your best supporting character."

"Brandon, I think you need to relax," Preston said with warning in his tone. Mitchell stepped up beside Preston.

"Brandon, I'm going to have to ask you to leave if you can't sit down, and calm down," Mitchell said sternly as he locked eyes with the slightly younger man. "We're all getting a little too excited."

Ida was blushing furiously as she looked over at Vicky. "There's something not right with that boy, I've said it for a while now. He's just too obsessed with these characters."

Vicky frowned as she studied Brandon from afar. She hadn't exactly been popular in high school and she had spent a lot of time with her nose in her favorite series. It was a lot easier than having to interact with others at the time. She wondered if Brandon felt the same way.

"I'm sure he's harmless," Vicky said softly and wrapped an arm around her aunt's shoulder. "But if he isn't, Mitchell will take care of it."

"All right, I'm sorry," Brandon growled out and dropped back down into his chair. He stared hard at the table.

"Actually, it's about time I wrap this up," Preston said with a smile. "The book launch will be starting in a few hours, and I like to be well rested when signing autographs."

The others in the group around him laughed lightly at his words, but Brandon just kept staring at the table in front of him.

"Oh, I'll show you to your room," Ida said and jumped up so suddenly that she nearly knocked right into Mitchell who was walking back towards Vicky with one eye still on Brandon. Mitchell caught Ida easily by the elbows and steadied her.

"Easy there," he murmured and met her eyes, his fierce blue gaze struggling to disguise his amusement.

"Oops," Ida blushed faintly and then straightened up.

"My dear," Preston offered her his arm and Ida happily took it. She cast a wink back at Vicky as she and Preston walked out of the restaurant.

"What do you think Rex is going to think of this?" Mitchell asked with a low chuckle.

"It's hard to tell what Rex is thinking," Vicky sighed, her gaze still lingering on Brandon. "But I know that Aunt Ida is having a grand time. Can't say the same for her friend, though."

"Yes, is he staying here?" Mitchell asked warily.

"He is," Vicky nodded. "Everyone from the group is since we're having a party after the book launch tonight. He is two rooms down from Preston actually."

"Well, we'll just have to keep a close eye on him," Mitchell frowned as he studied the young man. "I'll never understand people who idolize others like that."

"I can," Vicky smiled faintly. "It's nice to have a hero," she smiled up at Mitchell. "Someone you can rely on to be the good guy."

Mitchell grinned as he leaned down close to her and whispered beside her ear. "It's not always easy being the good guy."

Vicky laughed and kissed his cheek lovingly. They were so lost in their playful banter that neither noticed when Brandon crept out of the room.

Just as Mitchell was leaning in for a kiss, his cell phone began to ring. He hesitated and glanced down at it.

"Let me guess, our good friend Sheriff McDonnell?" Vicky asked with a heavy sigh.

"Mmhm," Mitchell replied before placing the phone to his ear. He kept his gaze locked on Vicky, as if he was hoping to pick up where he left off. "Yes Sir, I'm aware of the filing that needs to be done, Sir," Mitchell said into the phone and tried not to laugh. "Of course, I understand, not all police work is glamorous," he continued in the most polite of tones. "I just appreciate that you are so diligent ensuring that I will have a well-rounded experience."

Vicky had to cover her mouth to muffle her laughter. Whatever Sheriff McDonnell said next made Mitchell look away from Vicky. His amused expression faded.

"I'll be there in a few minutes," he said in a less polite tone. As he hung up the phone his lips drew into a tense line.

"Is something wrong?" Vicky asked with concern.

"Apparently my new responsibilities include cleaning the bathroom, and taking out the trash, because the janitor needed a night off," he raised an eyebrow as he looked back at Vicky. "Who knew the man could be so creative."

"You have the patience of a saint," Vicky said with a long sigh and a shake of her head. "I don't think I could take it."

"Well, he's not going to win," Mitchell said with confidence. "Now, where were we?"

Vicky smiled and kissed him lightly on the lips. "Until later, hmh?" she asked.

"Absolutely," he sighed and kissed her once more. She watched as he walked off through the lobby. She really did admire how patient he was, and respectful, even if she was ready to march right into Sheriff McDonnell's office and demand that he release her boyfriend.

Chapter Three

Vicky checked in with Sarah at the front desk to find that there was a little bit of chaos surrounding the book launch.

"Apparently there are going to be a few more reporters than we expected," Sarah said with a frown. "We're going to have to make sure they respect the privacy of our other guests."

"I can ask Sheriff McDonnell to send some officers over for security," Vicky offered with a mild shrug.

"Yes, I think that would be a very good idea," Sarah nodded and smoothed back her hair. "Who knew that Preston Price was so popular?"

"Aunt Ida," Vicky laughed as her aunt stepped out of the elevator. She had changed yet again and was adorned in a vibrant red dress that had more frills and lace than any dress Vicky had ever seen. She looked as if she was ready for a walk down the red carpet.

"Do you like it?" she asked her nieces as she spun in the middle of the lobby. "I thought it would be perfect for tonight."

"Looks good to me," Sarah nodded with approval.

"You look gorgeous," Vicky agreed. "And I'm not the only one who thinks so," she smiled as she tilted her head towards the front door of the lobby. A tall and burly man had just walked through the door. His gray, curly hair stood out against the black leather jacket he wore.

"Rex!" Ida said happily as she waved hello to him.

Rex had frozen just inside the door at the sight of Ida.

"Don't you look prettier than a fresh picked apple," he mumbled as his brown eyes widened.

Ida spun once more for him, and when she stopped, he had her in his arms.

"Why don't we go check on the banquet room to make sure it's ready," Vicky suggested and grabbed hold of Sarah's arm. Ida was like a mother to them both, and although they were glad that she had found happiness with Rex, it wasn't necessarily something that Vicky or Sarah wanted to witness.

***

The banquet room was set up correctly with the kitchen staff working quickly to ensure that the appropriate food and drinks were available. A central table was set up in the middle of the room where Preston would be seated.

"I've made three rows of chairs over here for the press," Sarah explained. "But I think we're going to need more like five, which is going to place us far too close to the food table."

"Well, we could stagger them like this," Vicky suggested as she angled a few of the chairs. "That way everyone has a good view and it doesn't block the food table."

"See, this is why I keep you around," Sarah said with a snap of her fingers.

"I hope it's not the only reason," Vicky laughed. Despite the fact that the sisters were quite different the bond between them had never been stronger.

"Give me some time, I'm sure I can come up with a few others," Sarah teased as she and Vicky placed the chairs. Once the chairs were set up Vicky checked on the kitchen a final time, and then headed back to her apartment to change. She pulled on a simple black dress, and fluffed her hair a bit. Then she crossed her fingers, and hoped that the launch would go off without a hitch. When she returned to the banquet room Preston was already there seated at his table with a stack of books beside him.

"Do you have everything you need?" Vicky asked as she paused beside the table.

"I think so," Preston nodded. "Ida has been very helpful."

"Oh I bet," Vicky laughed a little. "If you think of anything, just let me know."

"I will," he promised.

As Vicky walked away from him she noticed Brandon sitting in a corner. He had his legs crossed and his lips pressed tightly together. He didn't look as if he had calmed down at all from the last time she had seen him. She was just about to go over to talk to him when a group of reporters began filing into the banquet room. She escorted them over to their seats and offered to get them drinks. As she was organizing the reporters, the book launch began. Preston stood up in the middle of the room with the small microphone that had been provided.

"Thank you everyone for joining me in celebration of my latest title, 'Mysterious Mayhem'," Preston said with a smile to everyone in the room. All of the seats were occupied and there were a few more people standing. At the announcement of the title everyone applauded. "As you know, this is a very important book, it is crucial to the series. It reveals many secret details," he added as he looked around the room. "I hope that you will value it, as much as I valued the opportunity to write it."

"Hey," Mitchell whispered as he stepped into the room beside Vicky. "Thanks for requesting more police presence."

"Anything to hear that lovely accent," Vicky purred and winked at him.

Mitchell blushed and glanced over at Brandon. "Is he behaving himself?"

"So far," Vicky nodded.

After Preston had fielded several questions and read a passage from his book, he offered to sign autographs.

"I also have some special edition copies available," Preston explained. "So, if you don't have a copy of your own, you can always purchase one of these," he tapped the pile of books beside him. "It includes an alternative ending."

As the people in the room began lining up for autographs, Vicky lost track of Brandon in the crowd.

"I'm going to check the parking lot," Mitchell said quickly. "Just in case we have a lot of people trying to leave at once."

Vicky nodded distractedly. She was scanning the crowd for Brandon. As she stepped further into the crowd she finally spotted Brandon who was waiting next in line to speak to Preston. Vicky tried to push through the crowd to get close enough to Brandon to run interference if he should get out of hand as he had earlier. But before she could get to him, she saw Brandon smack his hand hard on the table.

"I want one of those copies," he insisted as he pointed to the single book that was left on the table.

"I'm sorry, this one wasn't supposed to be out here," Preston attempted to explain. "It was a mistake, I can't sell this copy."

"Or is it just because you are afraid I'll correct it?" Brandon glared furiously at him. Vicky reached the table, but Brandon had already stalked away.

"I'm sorry, Preston, I was trying to get over here," Vicky explained with a frown.

"It's quite all right," Preston assured her. "Brandon is just a little extra passionate."

"That's one way to put it," Vicky laughed a little. "Would you like me to stop the autographs?'

"No, it's fine, we can continue," he said and gestured to the next person waiting in line with a copy of his book. Vicky was relieved that Preston wasn't angry over Brandon's outburst, but she was getting more and more anxious about him being in the inn with Preston.

***

Once the launch was completed the party spilled out into the gardens, around the large pool, and into the small restaurant where there was a bar. It was quite a success, and Ida was right in the middle of it, being escorted by Rex. Vicky had to look twice when she saw him, as he looked very different in a suit, with his gray, curly hair in a neat braid down his back.

Preston was talking with his guests as he leaned against the bar. Everything seemed to be going very well. Vicky glanced at her watch. There was only about an hour left before the party would be shut down for the night. She didn't see any sign of Brandon at the party. She was finally beginning to relax. She caught a glimpse of Mitchell walking towards her through the crowd of people and smiled. He smiled in return and was nearly at her side when he was stopped by the ringing of his cell phone. He answered it, and then grimaced. Vicky crossed the distance between them as he was hanging up the phone.

"Don't tell me you have to go?" Vicky frowned as she looked into his eyes.

"I'm sorry," he murmured and kissed her forehead softly. "At least the money is good," he pointed out in an attempt to cheer her up.

"If it's about the money, Mitchell, I make plenty here, it's been a good year. I can help you out with whatever you need," Vicky said urgently. "Why not just tell him you're sick? Stay here with me?" she pleaded.

"It's not the money," he said firmly and met her gaze. "I need to do this, Vicky. If I cave in, he will think he has won, and then he will never respect me."

Vicky rolled her eyes and frowned. "Men are so weird."

"Yes," he tilted his head to the side. "Yes, we are. But at least we don't wear high heels. I don't think anyone could ever explain the sense in that to me."

"Ha ha," Vicky smiled and kissed him lightly. "All right if you must have your battle of wills fine, but you have to get some rest sometime."

"I will," he promised and kissed her once more.

Chapter Four

As the party wrapped up Vicky made sure the guests who were staying were able to get to their rooms, and those that were leaving were either sober enough to drive, or had a taxi to take them home. She was exhausted from the event but helped the staff tidy up the banquet room and restaurant. Once everything was shut down she instructed the kitchen staff to make sure that everything was locked up when they were finished with the last of the cleaning.

Vicky eagerly headed for her apartment and without much thought to changing collapsed into her bed. Somewhere in the back of her mind she wondered if Preston had made it to his room, and if Ida was safely nestled in her bed, but she was too exhausted to follow through on her curiosity. Just before she fell asleep she sent a text to Mitchell to tell him good night and that she loved him. It wasn't the same as snuggling up to him, but it would have to do for now.

Early the next morning she woke up to knocking on her door. Vicky's eyes were still blurry with sleep when she forced herself up out of her bed. She walked towards the door still trying to find her balance as the pounding continued.

"Who is it?" Vicky asked as she pulled open the door.

"Vicky," Ida said breathlessly as she pushed her way through the door.

"Aunt Ida, what's wrong?" Vicky asked.

"I can't find him," Ida said as she looked anxiously into Vicky's eyes.

"What do you mean? Rex? Who can't you find?" Vicky inquired.

"No, not Rex, Preston Price," Ida responded uneasily. "I think he might be missing!"

"Why?" Vicky frowned and rubbed at her eyes.

"I went to his room and knocked, but he didn't answer," Ida explained worriedly. "He had promised to join Rex and me for breakfast this morning."

"He may just have gone out for a morning run," Vicky suggested with a slight frown.

"Vicky, I think something may be wrong," Ida insisted. "Please, can you go up there and check in his room to make sure he's okay."

"All right, let me just get dressed," Vicky said and closed the door behind her aunt. Ida paced around the living room.

"Last night, he said he was an early riser like us and he would meet us at six-thirty this morning so we could take a walk and then we could take him to that breakfast place by the river," Ida explained as Vicky dressed. "But he didn't answer the door. I'm sure he wasn't in there. I'm sure he would have heard me if he was."

"I'm sure, too, if you were knocking as hard on his door as you were knocking on mine," Vicky said as she stepped back out of her bedroom. "But Aunt Ida, maybe he had a woman in the room with him, and just didn't want to answer," Vicky suggested.

"He's married, Vicky!" Ida said with a look of horror.

"And?" Vicky shrugged as she opened the door for Ida. "Some men don't take those vows too seriously."

"No, that's not Preston," Ida said with confidence. "He's a good man, loyal to his family."

"Aunt Ida, just because you've read all of his books doesn't mean that you know him," Vicky reminded her as she pushed the button for the elevator.

"I do know him," Ida insisted in return. "I'm sure he isn't in his room."

When they reached Preston's room Vicky knocked twice.

"Hello?" she called out. "Preston, are you in there?"

She waited a moment and heard no response.

"Vicky, I told you!" Ida explained. "Just open the door."

"Preston, I'm coming in!" Vicky warned. She hoped she wasn't going to walk into something she would rather not see. As she turned the key in the lock, she felt her heart skip a beat. All of a sudden all the things she might see on the other side of the door went sailing through her mind. Ida's wild imagination had rubbed off on her. She pushed open the door slowly and peered into the room. The small living area was empty and neat. The bed was empty. Vicky stepped further into the room.

"Preston?" she called out again. She walked over to the bathroom, knocked, and then opened the door. The bathroom was empty as well.

"Well, he's not here," Vicky said with a frown as she stepped back out of the bathroom.

"See, I told you," Ida sighed. "He's missing! Oh, I hope he's okay," she gasped out.

"Aunt Ida, he could have just gone out for some coffee, or even taken a walk around the gardens," Vicky pointed out.

"Without ever having slept in his bed?" Ida pointed to the bed which was still perfectly made from the day before.

"That is unusual," Vicky said with a nod. "But maybe he had a bout of insomnia, nervous about how the book would do, or too wound up from the party to sleep."

"Maybe," Ida sighed and walked back and forth across the carpet. "But something doesn't feel right about all of this."

"Maybe you're right," Vicky tilted her head towards the door. "Why don't we take a walk around the grounds and see if we can find him."

"Sure, let me just grab my sun hat," Ida said and headed off in the direction of the guest room that she stayed in.

Vicky took one more long look around Preston's room. It was very strange to her that there was no evidence that Preston had been in the room at all the night before. She hoped he hadn't decided to take off. If so, Aunt Ida would be very disappointed at not having had the chance to say goodbye.

As Vicky stepped out of the room and into the hallway she noticed a door two rooms down close very quickly. It took her a moment to remember that Brandon was staying in that room. As she walked past his room she paused for a moment and listened. It was completely silent inside. Then she heard a slow expelling of breath through the door. It sounded as if he was standing right on the other side, perhaps listening to see if she was still there. Vicky grew uneasy as she glanced back at Preston's room. She could only hope that her suspicions were unfounded, but that eerie sensation lingered all the way to the elevator.

***

Vicky met up with Ida in the lobby of the inn.

"I hope we can find him," Ida said as she wrung her hands nervously. "I promised the club that we would get one last chance to visit with him before he left."

"Hmm, maybe he decided to leave early," Vicky said thoughtfully. "Let me see if the night clerk might have checked him out."

As she walked behind the front desk to pull up the guest register on the computer, she was stopped short by a piercing scream from the direction of the restaurant. Vicky glanced at her watch. It should have just been opening for breakfast. She recognized the scream and fear carried from the tips of her toes to the top of her head before she could even move.

"Sarah!" she shouted as she raced across the lobby with Ida close on her heels. "Sarah?" Vicky cried out in a panic as she threw open the door of the restaurant and rushed inside. She saw Sarah standing in the middle of the restaurant, one hand covering her mouth, her eyes wide. Vicky grabbed her firmly by the shoulders and looked into her terrified eyes. "Are you okay, Sarah? What's wrong?" she asked.

Sarah raised one trembling hand and pointed her finger in the direction of the small bar that ran along the side of the central dining area of the restaurant. It was mostly available for wine and an occasional mixed drink for the guests. When Vicky looked in the direction that Sarah was pointing, her breath caught in her throat. Slouched over the bar, quite obviously dead from a bullet wound to the back of his head, was Preston.

"Oh no!" Aunt Ida gasped as she laid eyes on him.

Vicky turned and looked from her still shocked sister to Aunt Ida and then back to the body of the writer.

"Will you help me keep everyone out of here?" Sarah said in a daze to her aunt.

"I'll call Mitchell," Vicky said as Aunt Ida took Sarah's hand in hers to try and comfort her as they left the restaurant. Vicky swallowed thickly as she pulled out her cell phone and dialed Mitchell's number. He picked up on the first ring.

"Mitchell, I have a big problem," Vicky murmured into the phone, as if she was afraid that her voice might disturb the deceased. "That writer we had in for the weekend is dead in the restaurant."

"Please, tell me it was a heart attack or something?" Mitchell asked sleepily. Vicky frowned as she looked back at Preston's body.

"Not unless a heart attack can somehow cause a bullet wound to the back of the head," she replied anxiously. "Mitchell, this looks very bad. How soon can you be out here?"

"I'm on my way now," Mitchell assured her. "I'll call it in to Sheriff McDonnell," he added. "Vicky, be careful. Get out of the restaurant, keep the guests in their rooms. Until we figure out what this is about you have to consider that the shooter could still be in the inn."

"I'll be careful," she promised before she hung up the phone. She glanced around the restaurant which was dimly lit only by the sun filtering in through the windows. The restaurant hadn't been opened yet. The bar had closed at midnight the night before. She had done a walkthrough of the restaurant herself. No one had been in the restaurant when it closed. So, what was Preston doing in the restaurant in the middle of the night?

She carefully stepped closer to him, not wanting to disrupt any evidence that Mitchell might need to solve the crime. She noticed right away that his arms were stretched out across the bar. His hands were lodged in the thin metal railing behind the bar. Her heart pounded sharply as she remembered the discussion that Preston had with Brandon about the scene in his book that included a victim found in this exact position. She began to grow anxious as she recalled the door closing that morning as she left Preston's room. Had Brandon killed Preston? It was the only thing that made sense to her. But of course, it didn't really make any sense at all. Could Brandon have been so angered by Preston's disinterest that he thought it was reasonable to kill the man?

If that was the case, then Brandon might be planning to flee. Vicky ran out of the restaurant to find Sarah and Aunt Ida huddled close to the front desk. Sirens were shrieking outside the inn and the red and blue lights perched atop the police cars were painting strange murals on the walls of the lobby.

"Sarah, make an announcement call to each of the rooms and ask the guests to please stay in their rooms because there is an active police investigation," Vicky said as she glanced over at the elevator. "Has anyone left the building?"

"No, not since we've been out here," Sarah said as she walked behind the front desk to begin making the phone calls.

"I don't know how this could happen," Ida said in disbelief. "To think that if I had never invited him here, it never would have happened. It's all my fault."

"Aunt Ida, this was not your fault," Vicky said sternly and gave her aunt a quick hug. "We're going to figure out what happened, okay? I have to check on something, please show the officers where the crime scene is."

Ida nodded as Vicky walked away.

"Vicky, where are you going?" Sarah asked as she was making the first of many calls. "Vicky?" she called out when her sister ignored her and stepped into the elevator.

Vicky pulled out her phone and sent a text to Mitchell on the ride up in the elevator.

Think Brandon Derger might be the murderer, I'm checking to see if he's in his room now.

As expected her phone began to ring immediately, but she tucked it back into her pocket. She already knew what Mitchell was going to say. Wait for him, don't go near the suspect. But she wouldn't be able to live with herself if Brandon got away because she waited too long to check on him. If he was still in his room and tried to escape in the chaos of the police investigation then she might be able to distract him and stall him long enough for Mitchell to catch him. As she stepped out of the elevator she walked directly into Brandon.

"Ouch," he growled as Vicky had accidently stepped onto one of his feet. He shoved his glasses up and glared at her with annoyance. "If you'll excuse me," he said and tried to move past her into the elevator. Vicky noticed that he was carrying a small, brown bag in his hands. Her heartbeat quickened as she wondered if it might hold the murder weapon.

"I'm sorry, Brandon, we're asking all of the guests to remain in their rooms," Vicky said as she continued to block his way to the elevator. She knew that her sister and aunt were downstairs in the lobby. If Brandon was carrying a gun in that bag and got spooked by the police presence, he might just open fire.

"I got the call," he narrowed his eyes. "You can't keep me here against my will. I do not feel safe here, and I want to leave until things calm down. I'll be back later once the police have gone through this place. I have to go to the shops, anyway."

"If you'll just give us ten minutes or so," Vicky suggested as calmly as she could. "We want to give the police ample time to look over the inn and ensure the safety of everyone here."

"Ensure the safety?" Brandon chuckled. "Don't you think it's a little late for that?" he asked and shook his head. "I'm out of here," he laid his hand on Vicky's shoulder and began to shove.

"Take your hand off her right now and back away," Mitchell barked from the doorway that led to the stairs beside the elevator. He already had his gun drawn and was pointing it directly at Brandon.

"What is this about?" Brandon asked with disgust and fury as he drew his hand sharply away from Vicky. He raised his hands in the air as he stared down the barrel of Mitchell's gun. He still held the brown paper bag in his hands.

"He wasn't hurting me," Vicky said quickly. "But he has a bag with him and he was trying to leave."

Mitchell looked past Brandon just long enough to offer Vicky a look of disapproval that contained an entire lecture about putting herself in dangerous situations, before he looked back at Brandon.

"Drop the bag," he commanded him.

"No," Brandon replied sternly.

"Drop the bag," Mitchell repeated and took a step closer to Brandon.

"Look, I'll hand it to you, but I'm not going to drop it," Brandon said through gritted teeth. "Trust me, there's a good reason."

Vicky was even more certain that there must be a gun inside the bag. Maybe he was afraid that it would go off. Mitchell lowered his gun and reached for the bag. Once the bag was in his hands, he quickly opened it. Vicky subtly peered into the bag as Mitchell held it open. She expected to see a gun but inside there was no gun, instead there was a delicate glass figurine that Brandon had likely purchased from one of the tourist shops in town.

"No gun," she said quickly without thinking.

"Gun?" Brandon stammered out. "Why in the world would I have a gun?" he glared at Mitchell, and then at Vicky. "Is this how you treat all of your guests or did I get charged extra for the harassment package?"

"Watch it," Mitchell warned him as he stepped closer. "When was the last time you saw Preston?"

"Preston?" Brandon asked and furrowed his brow. "Do you mean the writer who doesn't respect his fans. The last time I saw him was at the book launch. I asked him for one of the special editions of his books, seeing as I am one of his biggest fans, and he refused. He said he didn't have any more. But there was one more on his table right in front of him. He just didn't want to give it to me. So, I told him that he had lost a fan and he could expect some scathing reviews, that was it," he shook his head as he looked between the two of them. "Is voicing my opinion a crime now?"

"We can discuss this further downstairs," Mitchell said as he curled his hand around Brandon's arm.

"You have no right to detain me," Brandon warned him.

"You're not being arrested, I just want to ask you a few questions," Mitchell added. "You were seen arguing with the victim, and you just told us how angry you were when he denied you a book you wanted."

"Wait a minute," Brandon said, his eyes wide. "Are you saying he's dead? Preston is dead?"

"Yes," Mitchell replied. "He has been murdered."

"Wow," Brandon shook his head slowly. "Who would think a murder mystery writer would end up the victim in his own murder mystery? It's quite brilliant really," he mumbled to himself.

"Murder is never brilliant," Mitchell muttered and escorted him into the elevator. Vicky stood in the hallway as the elevator doors slid shut. She caught sight of Mitchell's disgruntled frown when his eyes met hers. She knew he wasn't pleased that she had got into the middle of things, yet again.

Vicky frowned but headed back down the hall. She wanted to have a peek in Brandon's room before the police roped it off. As she slipped inside she noticed that everything was very tidy. The guests at the inn could be very messy, treating their room very differently than they would if they were at home. But Brandon had even made his own bed and his clothes were neatly folded in his suitcase.

Vicky noticed a stack of books on the bedside table. Each one had been written by Preston. She pursed her lips slightly as she wondered what it must have been like for Brandon to have his idol reject him in front of the entire book club. It just might have been enough for him to snap. As she peered around the room she noticed that there was a notebook lying open on the counter in the lounge room. On the page in tiny, neat handwriting, which she presumed was Brandon's, was a numbered list. Each item on the list seemed to be a detail or flaw in one of Preston's books. It was clear evidence of just how obsessive he was about the material that Preston had written.

"Vicky," Mitchell said from the doorway of Brandon's room. "You shouldn't be in here."

"I didn't touch anything," she promised as she turned to face him.

"Brandon's claiming he had nothing to do with the murder," he said with a frown as he carefully entered the room. His blue eyes were documenting everything he saw. Vicky adored the expression he would get when he was scrutinizing a crime scene.

"Well, I think the information in this notebook might indicate otherwise," Vicky said as she pointed to the notebook. "Is it possible to stalk a writer through his work?"

"I've heard of obsessed fans before," Mitchell grimaced as he looked over the list. "It usually doesn't end well."

"Maybe we should have paid closer attention to the way he was behaving at the book club meeting," Vicky said with a frown. "I saw him erupt at the launch, but I wasn't close enough to hear what he said."

"We couldn't have known," Mitchell shook his head and rubbed Vicky's shoulder lightly. "There's a big difference between someone who is passionate and someone who is obsessed, but sometimes they look very similar. None of this is your fault, understand?" he looked into her eyes intently.

Vicky nodded and then took a deep breath. "Well, at least all of this will be settled soon," Vicky shook her head. "The last thing we need is a media circus around the inn over this."

"I wouldn't be too sure about that," Mitchell said with a frown and ran his hand across the back of his neck.

"What do you mean?" Vicky asked nervously.

"Brandon claims he has an alibi, I'm waiting to see if it checks out," he shook his head. "The medical examiner places Preston's time of death at around one in the morning, Brandon said he was on the phone with a friend in Australia at the time. I've called to get the phone records."

"Well, he could have had his cell phone with him," Vicky pointed out. "Maybe he just kept the line open while he was committing the crime, to try to furnish an alibi for himself."

"It was from the phone in his room," Mitchell stated as he shook his head.

"Well, you can't put anything past him, Mitchell. He has practically lived inside these murder mysteries, if there is anyone who would know how to cover his tracks, it would be Brandon," Vicky frowned.

"Don't worry, we're going to hold him for some time," Mitchell assured her. "Even if his alibi checks out we can hold him for twenty-four hours for questioning."

"Good," Vicky nodded.

"I'm going to take him in and get started on the questioning," Mitchell added. "But in the meantime, just remain cautious. We don't know for sure it was Brandon, and until we do, the killer could still be lurking in the inn."

"I'll be cautious," Vicky promised him and kissed his cheek.

Chapter Five

Vicky found her aunt standing outside the restaurant. She watched as they rolled the stretcher out of the restaurant with Preston's body covered.

"How are you holding up, Aunt Ida?" Vicky asked as she wrapped an arm around her aunt's shoulders.

"I just can't believe he's dead," Ida admitted with tears in her eyes. "When I spoke to him last night he was so full of life." It wasn't often that Vicky saw her aunt looking so vulnerable and it brought a tear to her eye. She was usually so strong.

"It is shocking," Vicky agreed. "I'm sorry this happened."

"Me too," Ida sighed. "I wish I had paid more attention to what was happening before I left," she winced.

"Aunt Ida, they have Brandon Derger in custody," Vicky explained.

"Brandon?" Ida asked with surprise. "Why in the world do they have Brandon in custody?"

"What do you mean, why?" Vicky asked with confusion. "You saw the way he was behaving at the club meeting."

"Well, sure," Ida nodded, her eyes still wide. "But that's just Brandon. He's odd and he has his problems, but I can't ever imagine that he'd go this far."

"He's their best suspect right now," Vicky said as she led her aunt away from the restaurant. "Do you really think he wouldn't get angry enough to kill Preston?"

"I can't say for sure," Ida admitted. "He was obsessed with Preston, but I just can't picture him murdering Preston, not like that."

"I think it's the only lead they have right now," Vicky sighed. "But you may be right. He does claim that he has an alibi."

"I guess time will tell," Ida clucked her tongue a few times. "What a great loss, what a shame."

"I'm sorry again, Aunt Ida," Vicky hugged her gently. "Do you want to head over to Rex's while we figure all of this out?"

"Rex's? No way," Ida said and crossed her arms. "We have a mystery to solve, and I'm going to be here to solve it."

"All right, well I'm going to check in with Sarah about the guests, just let me know if you need anything, okay?" Vicky asked.

"Absolutely," Ida murmured, still dazed as she looked back towards the restaurant.

Vicky started to walk towards the front desk, when Ida reached out to stop her.

"Wait, Vicky," Aunt Ida grabbed her arm gently before she could walk away. "Think about this. In the book, the victim was killed the exact same way as Preston. If the murder was staged to look just like the murder in the book, then maybe it was committed the same way, too," Ida said with a hint of excitement growing in her voice.

"What do you mean?" Vicky asked curiously. "How was the murder committed?"

"A hit man shot the victim in the back of the head using a silencer," Ida explained as she shook her head. "The victim was found in the same position that Preston was, and was murdered around the same time. Whoever did this was very specific about how it was done. Maybe a hit man was hired to kill Preston, too."

"Hmm," Vicky nodded a little. "That might explain the lack of evidence. Mitchell mentioned that they didn't find so much as a fingerprint so far. A professional would be able to make a clean shot like that and not leave a trace behind."

"Oh dear," Ida frowned. "If that's the case then we may never find out who murdered Preston."

"Are you kidding, with all of us here!" Pamela asked as she walked up to them, the rest of the book club was following along behind her, aside from Brandon. "We have the best Murder Mystery Book Club just waiting to decipher all of the clues."

"I think it's best if we leave the investigation up to the police," Vicky said firmly. Ida peered at her out of the corner of her eye, but she stopped short of asking when the last time was that Vicky had stayed out of a police investigation.

"Oh please, isn't there something we can do?" Pamela asked urgently. "We are all his fans, we'd love to be part of solving this mystery."

"All right," Vicky finally nodded. "I'll tell you what you can do. Go through the newest book and tell me every little detail you can about the hit man. Also, get in contact with other fans and find out if anyone might have considered Preston an enemy. Perhaps they didn't like the twist the book took."

"You mean, anyone other than Brandon?" Pamela asked with narrowed eyes.

"They're looking into Brandon," Vicky assured her. "The police need all the information available. So, if you think you have any more information for them please feel free to contact this number," she said and handed Pamela one of Mitchell's cards. "He's the lead investigator on the case and he will listen to any information you have."

"Okay, I'll do that," Pamela nodded proudly. "Let's get to work, guys," she said and shooed the rest of the group into the nearby banquet hall. Ida followed after them and Vicky sighed with relief. She didn't want her aunt to be alone. She pulled out her phone and dialed Mitchell's number as she stepped out through the side door of the lobby. The small stone path led to the pool and the gardens.

"Aunt Ida thinks that it might have been a hired hit man like in the book," Vicky said into the phone as she walked through the gardens and towards the employee quarters. She wanted to double check to make sure that the officers had been able to find and question everyone that had been working the launch and after-party. She could feel her heart racing just at the sound of Mitchell's strained voice.

"Well, at this point that may be all we have to go on," he said with a sigh. "We checked into that phone call that Brandon claimed to have placed, and confirmed that he made it."

"That doesn't mean he couldn't have hired someone," Vicky pointed out. "It's a great way to give yourself an alibi. He's sitting in his room chatting away, while the murder is taking place."

"True," Mitchell agreed. "But any hit man worth his salt would be in the wind by now."

"Maybe," Vicky hesitated. "But, what if he didn't have a chance to disappear? He wouldn't want to be seen. Maybe he just decided to blend in with the crowd."

"You think he could still be at the inn?" Mitchell asked with urgency rising in his voice.

"Maybe," Vicky explained. "Maybe he stayed around to make sure all the evidence disappeared."

"Or her," Mitchell pointed out. "It could be a woman."

"Could be," Vicky replied with a sigh.

"Well, maybe you're right. He might have even booked a room at the inn. Why don't you go through the records of everyone that checked in, and compare it with the list of people that attended the launch party. If he was staying at the inn I'm willing to bet that this hit man would have checked in but not attended the party. He wouldn't want to risk that anyone remembers seeing him. So, maybe he hung out in his room until after the party."

"That's a great idea," Vicky agreed. "Most of our guests were here specifically for the launch so there can't be too many that didn't attend. I'll let you know if I find anything."

"Thanks, Vicky," Mitchell said warmly. "Remember..."

"Be careful!" Vicky returned in a knowing tone. "Don't worry, I will be," she promised him.

Vicky decided to skip talking to the employees and headed back to the lobby to check the computer. When she stepped back inside she was shocked at the crowd that had gathered in the lobby.

"Vicky!" Sarah waved her hand over her head behind the front desk. Vicky hurried over to her sister.

"What's going on?" Vicky asked as she looked at the tangle of guests.

"I just lifted the room restriction, and all these people want to check out. I guess that shouldn't surprise me, I just didn't expect them all to want to leave at the same time," Sarah cringed. "Can you help me with some of them?"

"Sure," Vicky nodded and took over the computer next to her sister's. While she was at it she pulled up the list of the people that had attended the launch and the after-party. She was checking out guests and offering a complimentary overnight stay while simultaneously checking the list. Finally, she came to a name that appeared on the guest register but was not listed as attending the launch or the party. Lyle Cole. She frowned as she studied the name for a long moment, trying to jog her memory. She couldn't put a face to the name at all.

"Here you are, Mr. Cole," Sarah was saying as she handed him a voucher for his free overnight.

"No thanks, I won't be needing it," he muttered casually and instantly disappeared into the crowd. Vicky ducked out from behind the desk and tried to follow him, but there was a sea of faces to look through.

Finally, Vicky noticed the young man standing at the edge of the group of people who were walking out of the inn. Sarah was still drowning in guests that wanted to check out. But one was getting a bit irate.

"I checked my jewelry into the safe," the woman was saying. "I have the slip right here."

"All right, let me just get that for you," Sarah assured her and ducked into the office to retrieve it.

Vicky knew Sarah would be upset if she left the desk unmanned, but she also knew that she couldn't let a potential hit man get away. She watched as he glanced down at his watch, and then reached up to scratch at the tattoo of a ring of thorns that was nearly hidden beneath the collar of his shirt. Vicky was getting more and more convinced that this had to be the hit man, even though she had never laid eyes on him before. Sarah must have been the one to check him in. It wasn't the tattoo that made her so certain, it was the way he moved. Each gesture was made with precision and an eerie emotionless calm. She knew that if he got out the door they might never capture him.

Vicky texted Mitchell the name of the potential suspect, but got no response. She tried calling Sheriff McDonnell but he didn't answer, either. She knew she had to do something to prevent him from leaving, but she couldn't figure out what. If she tipped him off to the fact that she suspected him, he might bolt or even hurt someone. Mitchell's warnings to be cautious echoed in her ears, but was it her fault that Mitchell wasn't picking up the phone? She gritted her teeth as she watched the man moving closer to the door. She walked towards him, doing her best not to look directly at him. He was glancing around now and then, casually. If she didn't suspect who he was, she wouldn't have thought that it was suspicious.

"Excuse me," she said quietly to a couple that was blocking her way. Lyle looked up when he heard her voice. Briefly their eyes met before he looked quickly away.

Vicky could only hope that he didn't know who she was. If Sarah had checked him in, he might not know that she was Sarah's partner in the inn. The desk had been so busy that he probably hadn't even looked in her direction. As she crept closer to him, he seemed to inch further away. Then Vicky noticed the tension ripple through his shoulders. She knew that he was getting ready to bolt.

"Excuse me!" Vicky waved her hand wildly and looked directly at Lyle. Lyle looked up at her with alarm, but Vicky pretended to be waving to the man in front of him, who was blocking the door with his suitcase. "Excuse me!" she called out. "I think you dropped your wallet!" she said. The man stopped, as she had hoped he would and began digging through his pockets to check to see if he had his wallet. Vicky knew she only had a few moments before he would realize he did indeed have his wallet and that she was mistaken. In those moments she had to act quickly.

"Excuse me," she said as she came to stand right beside Lyle. She reached out to lean on the door and when she did, she pushed the slide lock.

"I have my wallet right here," the man sighed and shook his head. "It must belong to someone else."

"I'm so sorry," Vicky said with a frown. Her heart was pounding heavily. She knew that she had just put herself and everyone else who was still inside the lobby at risk.

"It's all right," the man said and pushed on the door, expecting it to open. Instead the door would not budge.

"Uh oh," he said as he shoved hard at the door. "It must be stuck."

"Here, let me try," Lyle said with annoyance and shoved hard at the door. "Why won't it open?" he demanded and shoved harder.

"Here let me take a look," Vicky said, purposefully guiding the other guest out of the way so that he was at a safe distance from Lyle. She wiggled the handle on the door, pretending not to know why it wouldn't budge.

"Would you hold this?" she asked Lyle as she gestured to the door handle. She watched as his large hands passed over hers and pressed the handle of the door.

"Oh, those waiting can use the side door," she gestured to the door off to the side of the lobby. As the other guests began heading for the other door, Lyle started to let go of the handle of the door to follow them.

"If you don't mind could you just hold it a moment or two longer?" Vicky pleaded as she pretended to struggle with the door.

"I really need to go," Lyle growled and she could tell that he was getting suspicious of her intentions. She glanced over at the other guests and watched as the last left through the side door. Then she looked back at Lyle.

"What's this?" he said as his fingertips grazed the slide lock hidden beneath the handle of the door. "Did you lock this?" he asked and glowered at her with increasing anger.

"Oh, is it locked?" Vicky continued to do her best to play innocent. She could only hope that Mitchell would get her text and arrive very soon.

"Are you playing some kind of game here?" Lyle asked. His hands left the handle of the door and grabbed onto Vicky's wrists roughly.

"Let go!" Vicky cried out as she tried to pull her hands free.

"Nothing is stopping me from leaving," he warned her sharply and began to twist her wrists painfully. Vicky's knees threatened to buckle under the force of the twisting.

In the next second Lyle was laying flat on his back, gurgling on the floor, with Ida's foot planted squarely on his chest. She had moved so fast that Vicky barely saw her wrap her arm around Lyle's neck, jerk him backwards and flip him over her right leg.

"Are you okay, Vicky?" Ida asked with concern.

"Yes," Vicky replied as she rubbed lightly at her wrists. "I think this might be the hit man," she whispered to Aunt Ida as she continued to rub her wrists.

They were sore but not broken. She heard rattling and turned to see Mitchell trying to force the door open. Quickly she slid the lock free and he pushed the door open immediately. He looked from Vicky, to Ida, and then to Lyle still pinned and struggling for breath on the floor. He was silent as he crouched down and flipped Lyle over to handcuff him. But when he looked up at Vicky she could see the mixture of concern and impatience in his eyes. After reading Lyle his rights he handed him over to another officer and walked over to Vicky.

"Did he hurt you?" he asked, his voice heavy with barely restrained fury.

"No, not really," Vicky replied as she folded her hands behind her back.

"Let me see," he requested with one eyebrow raised.

She sighed and extended her hands. Her wrists were still red, but it didn't look to Vicky like they would bruise.

Mitchell ran his fingertips lightly along the injuries in a soothing manner. "Wouldn't have happened if you had waited..." he began to lecture.

"He would have gotten away!" Vicky pointed out with a frown. "I did call and text."

"I'm sorry," he frowned as he let his hands fall away. "I was in the interrogation room with Brandon. I never have my cell with me in there."

"Don't worry, she had back up," Ida said with a smile and carefully fluffed her hair.

Mitchell couldn't help but smile at her words. "That's true, it's always good to know that Vicky has her own personal bodyguard."

"I could have handled it," Vicky insisted but she opened her arms to her aunt. "But as always, you're my hero, Aunt Ida. Without you being here I'm sure Lyle would have got away."

"Well, it's a good thing we caught him," Ida said as she hugged Vicky. "But that still doesn't explain who hired him presuming he is the hit man."

"Once I get a chance to talk to him, I should be able to get more information out of him," Mitchell said with confidence.

"Can I come and observe?" Vicky asked hopefully. She loved to watch Mitchell at work. It wasn't often she had the chance to.

Mitchell hesitated, and then he nodded. "Actually you can. Sheriff McDonnell is home for the day. But you have to stay out of sight," he warned her.

"That, I can do!" Vicky assured him. "Let me just finish helping Sarah with the last of the guests who are checking out and I'll meet you over there."

"Okay," Mitchell nodded.

"Oh, I can help Sarah," Ida insisted. "You two go ahead. You can have a few moments in the car together," she smiled warmly.

"Thanks, Aunt Ida," Vicky said and gave her aunt's hand a squeeze before following Mitchell to his car.

***

As Vicky and Mitchell drove to the police station, Vicky felt the tension building between them. It was a pleasant tension, instigated by Mitchell lightly resting his hand over hers, and the stolen glances they kept passing in each other's directions. Vicky cleared her throat and tried to focus on the investigation.

"Do you really think he's going to tell you the truth?" Vicky asked as she studied Mitchell.

"I think he's going to want to," Mitchell replied as he glanced over at her. "I can be quite persuasive, after all."

"That's true," Vicky smiled. "But I don't think sweet talk is going to work on Lyle."

"Who said anything about sweet?" Mitchell asked as he pulled into the parking lot of the police station. "Lyle's not going to know what hit him, trust me," he said as he parked the car. He stepped out and opened Vicky's door for her. Mitchell was always a gentleman, it was something that Vicky was becoming accustomed to. The little gestures really did add up.

As they stepped into the police station, Mitchell glanced around to be certain that Sheriff McDonnell wasn't present and then escorted Vicky into a holding room on the other side of the interrogation room. It had a two-way mirror that revealed Lyle already seated in the interrogation room.

"I am going to see if I can get any information on him and then question him," Mitchell explained. "If anyone asks you why you're in here, tell them to speak to me about it," he said firmly. Vicky wasn't too worried about it as she had gotten to know the other officers fairly well, and they all liked and respected Mitchell.

"Got it, get to work," Vicky said and tipped her head towards the mirror.

Mitchell nodded and stepped out of the room. Vicky watched Lyle staring aimlessly at the mirror. Vicky suspected he knew that someone was standing on the other side. He carried on staring for some time until Mitchell appeared in the interrogation room.

"So, Lyle or should I say Frank, who hired you?" Mitchell asked as he sat down across from him.

"I don't know what you're talking about," Lyle replied coolly and stared hard at Mitchell. Vicky found it a little unnerving to see Mitchell alone in the room with someone she suspected was a vicious criminal. Even though she knew that Lyle was cuffed and Mitchell was armed as well as being a very capable police officer, she couldn't take a breath as Mitchell leaned closer to Lyle.

"I have run a check and I know that you real name is Frank Glost. Lyle Cole is just an alias. But I will call you Lyle if that's what you prefer. Whatever I call you it won't change the fact that you're going to prison for a very long time," Mitchell said as he narrowed his eyes. "We matched the bullet from Preston's body, to the bullets still in the chamber of your gun. You have a long history of violent crimes for hire. It is clear that you were involved in this murder. But I don't think you did it alone. I think someone paid you to do it," he paused a moment and sat on the edge of the table near Lyle. "I can tell from your history that you're a professional, Lyle. I know this crime was nothing personal. You know as well as I do, that if you give me the information on who hired you, your sentence is going to be much lighter. So, let's just skip the lies, give me the information I need."

"Why should I?" Lyle smirked as he looked up into Mitchell's eyes. "You think I'm going to care if my sentence is ten years of thirty? It doesn't matter."

"It might matter if it's life," Mitchell replied darkly. "I've got you on murder for hire, assault, and assault and battery of a senior citizen."

"What?" Lyle growled. "That old bitty took me down! I didn't lay a hand on her!"

"And you want that advertised in court?" Mitchell asked with a slight chuckle. "How do you think your buddies in prison are going to treat you when they find out that you tried to beat up an old lady, and she was the one who had you pinned to the ground?"

Lyle frowned and lowered his eyes. It was clear that he had some not so fond memories of being in prison before.

"So, maybe if you tell me who hired you, I'll let a few of those charges slide," Mitchell said casually. "But it needs to be all of the information. Because you committed a serious offence in my jurisdiction."

Vicky smiled as she looked through the mirror. She loved watching Mitchell work and the way he was protective of the people in the town. She only hoped he would be able to get Lyle to talk.

"All right, all right," Lyle finally shook his head. "I don't get paid enough for this," he sighed. "The guy's name is Kevin Price, he hired me to off his brother. Uh, Preston Price," he muttered and shifted in his chair.

"Preston Price's brother hired you to kill him?" Mitchell said with disbelief. "Why?"

"Hey man, I don't ask questions," he said with a scowl. "A man pays me for a job, I do it. They must have had some kind of beef though. He was real funny about things. Everything had to be done a certain way, at a certain time, or he said he wasn't going to pay me the other half of my money. That's why I was still at the inn. He was supposed to pay me the second half after the body was found. But he didn't show up, I figured it was all the heat."

"Do you have any idea where he is now?" Mitchell pressed hopefully.

"Wherever he is, he better be running, because nobody stiffs me. He owes me half the payment," he shook his head.

"Well, I don't think you're going to have to worry about that for some time," Mitchell said with disgust.

"Don't forget about my deal," Lyle reminded him quickly.

"Huh?" Mitchell asked as he backed out of the room. He closed the door against the string of curses that Lyle let loose.

Chapter Six

While Mitchell was hunting down Preston's brother, Ida picked up Vicky from the police station. Aunt Ida still had a motorbike which she loved to take on the open road but she kept her car for emergencies, like carrying bags when she had been on a shopping spree. On the car ride back to the inn Vicky filled her in on what Lyle had said.

"So, there was really a hit man hired," Ida said with shock in her voice. "It's all so unreal. That fiction could be brought to life in such a way."

"I just can't believe that a brother could do that to a brother," Vicky said softly. "Sarah's my best friend, and more than that, she's one of the few people I trust with anything and everything. I can't imagine what could ever happen between siblings to drive someone to that point."

"Well, you're lucky," Ida said quietly as she gazed out of the window. "You and Sarah have had some hard knocks, but you've always had each other, and that makes a difference. Sometimes siblings do the opposite, they pull apart, even attack each other."

"We've had you, too," Vicky reminded her aunt gently. "If you weren't there to help us, I don't know what would have happened."

"You would have been fine," Ida said with confidence. "But of course, you'd have less entertaining company."

"There's one thing I can't understand," Vicky said with a frown. "Lyle was here for the book launch. He said that Kevin asked to meet him here. Why would Kevin come all the way here to hire him?"

"Maybe to make sure that he could arrange the perfect murder?" Ida suggested. "It's not as easy as they make it look in the books, you know."

"But he risked getting caught," Vicky pointed out. "Anyone could have seen him talking to Kevin."

"Actually," Ida said softly. "I was too busy knocking that hooligan on his back to pay much attention to his face, but now that I think about it, I'm pretty sure I did see him at the inn," she paused and frowned.

"You did?" Vicky asked quickly. "Did you see who he might have been talking to?"

"I remember," Aunt Ida said thoughtfully. "It was on the first day that Preston arrived. After I showed him around he excused himself. I admit I was a little curious, so I followed him. He put on his hat and sunglasses and went out into the parking lot. That's where I saw Lyle, he was in the parking lot waiting for Preston. They talked for a few minutes at the corner of the lot. Then Preston handed him a package. I just figured that the man was a fan, and Preston was giving him a special edition book like he had given me. It was in the same type of packaging."

"And you're sure that it was Lyle?" Vicky asked as she studied her aunt intently. "Is it possible that you were mistaken and it might have been someone else?"

"Yes, I'm sure," Ida nodded. "I remember because of his tattoo, I thought it was interesting. I was going to ask him who the artist was, because I might get another, but he walked away so fast when Preston left that I figured it would be rude to chase after him. I didn't want Preston to think that I was stalking him," she added with a light laugh.

"No more tattoos," Vicky said sternly. "But if you really did see Preston speaking to Lyle, that doesn't make sense. If Lyle was the hit man hired to kill Preston, why would Preston be giving him a package?"

"I don't know," Ida sighed as she pulled into the parking lot of the inn. "Maybe he found out. Maybe he was hoping to pay off the hit man to prevent his own death."

"Why wouldn't he just go to the police?" Vicky pointed out and narrowed her eyes. "No, something sure doesn't add up."

"I agree," Ida nodded as she turned off the car. "I'll check in with the group to see if they came across anything."

"Okay," Vicky murmured as she stepped out of the car. She dialed Mitchell's number as Ida disappeared inside the inn.

Mitchell answered quickly with a touch of frustration in his tone.

"I have some more information for you," Vicky said quickly.

"Good," Mitchell sighed. "Because I'm not getting very far. We've found Kevin, Preston's brother, but there's nothing to indicate he would have hired Lyle.

In fact, we have no way to prove that a transaction even took place."

"Well, according to Aunt Ida, she saw Preston in the parking lot with Lyle, handing a package to him," Vicky explained quickly.

"That doesn't make any sense," Mitchell groaned.

"That's what I said," Vicky agreed. "But she saw Lyle's tattoo. Is that enough to identify Lyle?" she asked hopefully.

"It is," Mitchell said with an uncomfortable tone of voice. "But it just doesn't add up, does it? Why would Preston be meeting with the hit man who was hired to kill him?"

"Well, maybe he didn't know he was the hit man," Vicky suggested. "Maybe he thought he was just a fan."

"Vicky!" Ida called out as she came running back out of the inn. "I remember why it was so strange to me," Ida said with wide eyes. "We need to get Brandon to help us."

"Brandon?" Vicky asked with surprise. "Why?"

"It'll be much faster than searching through the book, just trust me," Ida insisted.

"All right," Mitchell said into the phone as Ida had been loud enough for him to overhear. "I'll be there in a few minutes, see if you can track down Brandon."

"I will," Vicky agreed and hurried with her aunt into the inn. She nearly walked right into Brandon who was trying to force his way out through the door.

"Brandon, just who we need to see," Ida said cheerfully.

"What? Why?" Brandon growled and glared at both of them. "I can't wait to put this whole weekend behind me."

"Wait Brandon, I want to give you the chance to help out with the case, and to clear your name," Ida said with a knowing smile. Brandon would not be able to resist being involved in the case.

"What are you thinking, Aunt Ida?" Vicky asked as she watched her aunt guide Brandon back into the lobby.

"If I'm not mistaken, there is something very, very strange happening here," she shook her head and stopped pacing as Brandon crossed his arms and stood by her side.

"Obviously," Brandon rolled his eyes.

"Brandon, in the book, didn't the person who hired the hit man wear sunglasses and a hat?" Ida asked with urgency in her voice.

"Yes, which was ridiculous as far as disguises go because it wasn't even a sunny day, and sunglasses don't hide much," he paused a moment and narrowed his eyes. "Why?"

"I saw Preston in the parking lot wearing a hat and sunglasses, talking to the man who we think was hired to kill Preston," Ida explained quickly. "Why would Preston do that?"

"Preston?" Brandon shrugged mildly. "Well, if I were Preston, and I knew someone had taken a hit out on me, maybe I would be trying to take out a hit on that person instead. I mean, hit men are mercenaries, they will do whatever they're asked for the right price."

"So, you think Preston was paying the hit man off?" Ida pressed as Vicky opened the door to the lobby for Mitchell. "But why did Preston end up dead then?" Vicky asked.

"Maybe because of this," Mitchell said as he displayed a photograph on his cell phone.

"Because of his ruggedly handsome good looks?" Ida asked with annoyance as she looked at the picture.

"That's not Preston," Mitchell explained and raised his eyebrows. "That's his brother Kevin. They look so similar they could almost be twins, hmm?"

"Absolutely," Vicky gasped.

"Oh wow, an evil twin," Brandon rubbed his hands together swiftly. "Even I didn't see that coming."

"It's as if someone has painstakingly recreated the murder right out of Preston's book. Who could do such a thing?" Ida shook her head with disbelief.

"I could," Brandon said with a frown. Then his eyes widened as he held up his hands. "But I didn't, I didn't," he insisted as he looked over at Mitchell.

"So, who would know as much as Brandon?" Ida asked in a murmur.

"The writer," Vicky suddenly announced. "Preston would know so many of the details."

"But again, that makes no sense," Mitchell said with a soft growl. "How could Preston plan out his own murder?"

"Maybe he didn't mean for it to be a murder," Vicky suggested abruptly. "Maybe this was all staged to draw publicity to his book. Maybe it was just supposed to be a stunt, but then something went wrong."

"Maybe," Mitchell replied and ran his hand along his chin. "That would make a little more sense. But how could things have gone wrong?"

"Hey, I know this might not be the right time," Brandon cleared his throat. "But remember that last book that Preston had? If no one's going to take it, I'd be happy to pay for it."

"Not the right time, Brandon," Ida chastised and shooed him out of the room.

Vicky frowned as she started thinking about the book. It was very strange. Why didn't Preston want to give away the book? Her thoughts were interrupted by Mitchell's voice.

"I'll see if I can get some information out of Kevin. If he looks so similar to his brother, he might have been the one that Ida saw in the parking lot. Maybe he really did hire Lyle to kill his brother, and thought he would get away with it because no one would recognize him."

"That's a good point," Vicky said. "I never thought of it that way. Aunt Ida, do you think it's possible you lost sight of Preston long enough for it to have actually been Kevin that you saw put on a hat and sunglasses?" she asked.

Ida thought for a moment and then slowly nodded. "I guess it is possible," Ida frowned.

Chapter Seven

Vicky kept thinking about the book Preston refused to give Brandon at the launch. After telling Aunt Ida her thoughts about the book they decided to try and find it. Preston's room was as clean and tidy as it had been when Vicky and Ida first looked it over when they couldn't find him. But now there was police tape roping it off, and a few things had been taken for evidence. Vicky ducked under the tape and then held it up for Ida to step in behind her. Once inside she looked around the room.

"Where would he have stashed it?" Ida said softly as she swept her gaze over the room.

"If the book was important to him he probably would have kept it close," Vicky suggested and walked over to the bed. She lifted the blanket to peer underneath. There was nothing to be found, not even a dust bunny, as the maids were very thorough. As she straightened back up she noticed that a leg of the bed frame was shifted out of place slightly. Not enough to disrupt the look of the bed, but enough to indicate that it had been moved recently. She got down all the way on her hands and knees and ran her hand along the underside of the bed. Wedged between the mattress and the frame was a book. She pulled it out carefully.

"I've got it," she said to Ida who was still scouring the room.

"What's in it?" Ida asked with a hint of excitement.

Vicky flipped the book open. She was expecting something, maybe a photograph, maybe a detailed list of the plan, but instead all she saw were the uniform pages of a book.

"There's nothing," she said quietly with a slow shake of her head.

"There must be something," Ida insisted and took the book from Vicky. She flipped through the pages three times. "There really is nothing," she said with defeat. "Why in the world would anyone hide a book under their bed if there was nothing special about it," she frowned as she flipped a corner of a page that had been folded over back up. "I hate when people do this to books," she clucked her tongue. "A simple bookmark can hold a place better than bending the page."

"Aunt Ida, I think we have bigger things to be concerned about," Vicky reminded her as she stood up. Then she suddenly looked back at the book. "Wait a minute, is that the only page that's turned down?"

"No," Ida sighed. "There's a bunch of them, and on a collector's edition," she clucked her tongue again as she began smoothing another corner.

"Aunt Ida, stop!" Vicky suddenly said.

"What?" Ida asked with surprise as she looked up at her niece.

"What if that's a clue," Vicky said as she took the book back from her aunt. "Maybe there's something on the pages that will tell us what happened."

"Hmm, maybe," Ida shook her head with a smile of admiration. "You're so very clever, Vicky."

"None of this makes sense," Vicky scanned the text. "It's bits and pieces of all different scenes. The only thing similar about the pages is that they have print, and page numbers."

"I'm sorry, Vicky, maybe if we let Mitchell have a look," Ida suggested with a mild shrug.

"The page numbers," Vicky repeated as she stared down, nearly mesmerized. "How many are there," she muttered to herself. Ida watched her intently as Vicky flipped through all the folded down corners. "That's it!" she gasped out and looked up at Ida with wide eyes. "There are ten numbers, the same amount of numbers in a phone number. I bet it's a phone number!"

"Why in the world would he go to all that trouble when he could have just jotted a number in the cover or a margin?" Ida asked with confusion.

"Because it was that important to hide it," Vicky said with confidence. "He didn't expect anyone to look at the book, but if they did, he didn't want anyone to find the phone number scrawled inside it."

"Well, if that's what you really think, then let's call it," Ida said eagerly.

Vicky pulled out her cell phone, and then hesitated. "No, we should tell Mitchell first. He'll want to check the number in the system."

"Aha, being a good girl," Ida winked. "Let's go show him then."

"Whoever this phone number belongs to might just be able to solve this mystery," Vicky said with some excitement.

***

When Vicky and Ida arrived at the police station Mitchell took a moment to greet them.

"I think we found something important," Vicky said as she held the book out to him. "I think this is the special edition that Preston wouldn't give to Brandon."

"A book?" Mitchell asked and quirked a brow. "How is this important?"

"It's important because of the page numbers," Vicky explained, and then faltered slightly. At the time she had discovered it, it had seemed like such a great idea. But now that she was explaining it, she felt a little silly. "I think they make up a phone number."

"Oh," Mitchell nodded as he thumbed through the book. "What makes you think that?"

"I'm not sure," Vicky sighed and blushed a little. "I'm sorry, it's just a hunch."

Mitchell pulled out his cell phone, and Vicky was sure that he had no interest in her theory as he thumbed through his phone. "Don't worry about it, Mitchell, it's probably nothing," she said quickly.

Mitchell looked up at her as he put the phone to his ear. "Vicky, there's no harm in testing you're hunch," he smiled a little. Suddenly a phone began ringing at Mitchell's desk.

"Oh, well look at that," Mitchell said as he raised his eyebrows. He walked over to his desk quickly.

"Did you call the number?" Ida asked as she and Vicky followed after him.

"Yes I did, and this is the phone it went to," Mitchell said as he picked up an evidence bag with a phone inside.

"Whose phone is it?" Vicky asked urgently.

"Lyle's," Mitchell replied as he hung up his cell phone.

"What?" Ida and Vicky both said at the same time.

"How can everything in this murder be pointing at the victim hiring a hit man?" Vicky asked incredulously.

"Maybe we're missing something," Mitchell said as he began to pace and rub at his chin. Vicky was slightly distracted as she watched him move so lithely. Whenever he was focused very deeply he seemed to prowl.

"Let's take a step back," Vicky suggested and took a literal step back. "Now, we know that we found the book with the hit man's phone number underneath Preston's bed. We also know that Lyle met with someone in the parking lot."

"He met with Preston," Mitchell corrected as he came to a standstill.

"Do we know that?" Vicky asked curiously. "What if he was meeting with someone who just looked like Preston."

"Like his brother, Kevin?" Mitchell said with widening eyes. "That does make sense, Vicky. They look similar enough. With a hat and some sunglasses, he could easily have disguised himself as his own brother."

"But what kind of brother hires someone to kill his brother?" Vicky frowned and shoved her hands into her pockets. "That's what I can't seem to get past. Poor Preston, he had no idea what he was up against."

"I think it's time I had a nice long conversation with Kevin," Mitchell said as he made a note in his notebook and then looked up in the direction of the door as two policeman walked in with Kevin. "Uniforms are bringing him in now."

"This is the most confusing case," Vicky sighed. She grabbed his hand lightly in her own. "But to be honest it's so nice getting to spend some time with you."

"Yes, it is," he replied and smiled for a moment, but his smile faded. "Too bad someone has to be murdered for us to get some alone time."

Vicky grimaced at that comment. "Yes, that's not exactly romantic, is it?"

"Not at all," Mitchell shook his head. "We're going to have to change that," he breathed out his words as he took a step closer to her. "Soon."

Vicky searched his eyes for a hint of what he might be planning, but he only winked and walked away. She stared after him for a moment before walking out of the police station. She met Ida in the parking lot where she was talking to Rex.

"I don't think you should get too wound up in all of this," Rex warned Ida as Vicky walked up. "I don't want you getting hurt."

"Me? Get hurt?" Ida laughed at the idea. "Haven't I told you about my black belt?"

"A black belt won't always work against a gun, Ida," he reminded her sternly. Vicky paused respectfully beside them.

"Ah Vicky, will you please inform my beau that I am perfectly capable of protecting myself," Ida said impatiently.

"She's saved me a few times," Vicky laughed a little.

"See?" Ida said indignantly.

"That doesn't mean I don't get to worry," Rex growled. "Once this is all over, I'm taking you on a road trip. We're going to have a nice get away from all of this business."

"That sounds like a lovely idea," Ida agreed.

"Do you know who the man is that was just escorted into the police station?" Rex asked inquisitively.

"I think it was Preston's brother, Kevin. Why do you know him?" Vicky asked as she studied Rex.

"No," he shook his head. "But, I think I saw him the day of the launch. He was standing outside smoking a cigarette. I thought it was the writer at the time but maybe it was his brother. They look very similar."

"No way it was Preston, he doesn't smoke," Ida shook her head firmly. "I would have smelled it on him."

"It must have been Kevin," Vicky said with widened eyes. "That means he was at the inn. Which means he might have been the one in the parking lot meeting with Lyle and arranging his brother's death."

"How terrible," Ida sighed and looked away. "To think Preston's life has been ended by someone he should have been able to trust."

"Vicky?" Sheriff McDonnell asked as he walked towards the front door of the police station. "What are you doing here?" he narrowed his eyes.

"I'm sorry, I was just dropping by to see if I could steal a moment with Mitchell," Vicky explained quickly as Ida and Rex took off on Rex's motorcycle.

"Oh, I see," he nodded slightly. "So you'd have nothing to do with the generous amount of information Mitchell has been able to discover in such a short period of time about a high profile case?" he asked.

"I uh," Vicky hesitated and glanced away. She wasn't sure what the penalty was for lying directly to the Sheriff, but she was certain she didn't want to pay it.

"Relax," Sheriff McDonnell laughed a little. "I know it was you helping out. I also know that this case is not adding up for anyone involved. It is great that you can provide such detailed information of where the crime occurred."

"Of course, anything you need," Vicky offered with relief. She hadn't wanted to get Mitchell into trouble by interfering.

"Okay, in fact, why don't you join me?" he opened the door to the police station inviting her to step in before him. Vicky stared at him for a moment. She couldn't be certain that this wasn't some kind of trick.

"Okay," she replied finally and stepped inside. He led her back past the rows of desks to the interrogation rooms.

"Why don't you listen in. Maybe you'll pick up on something," he lowered his voice slightly as he opened the door to the other side of the interrogation room where she would be able to observe once more through the two-way mirror. "As soon as the case is solved, I'll make sure Mitchell gets a day off, all right?"

"All right," Vicky said with surprise. She couldn't figure out exactly what Sheriff McDonnell was up to. He seemed to change moods so quickly. But she wasn't going to argue with him. She was very excited at the possibility of a day with Mitchell. She stepped up to the mirror and watched the interrogation that was already taking place.

"This is ridiculous," Kevin said as he stared at Mitchell. "I did not hire a hit man to kill my brother."

"Where were you this weekend?" Mitchell asked sharply.

"I was here in Highland!" Kevin said with exasperation. "Preston called me. He said he wanted to settle things between us and to meet him at the launch. So, I flew all the way here. It was stupid, I actually thought he meant it," he shook his head and lowered his eyes.

"Where were you the night of your brother's murder?" Mitchell pressed, his expression hardening. When he got angry his blue eyes grew fierce, it was something that still took Vicky by surprise.

"I was right where you found me!" Kevin gasped out. "I was supposed to fly out but there was some kind of problem with my ticket and they wouldn't let me on the flight. So, I had to spend the night at the airport."

"With no one to confirm that you were there?" Mitchell asked with disbelief in his tone. "That sounds like a pretty thin alibi to me."

"There were other people there, security, and passengers," Kevin trailed off, as if he knew that those witnesses would never be able to single him out from the crowd. "Oh, this is all so crazy," he sighed and rubbed his forehead.

"You said that you had something to straighten out with your brother," Mitchell continued. "Was that the lawsuit you filed against him?"

"You know about that?" Kevin asked nervously as he looked up at Mitchell. "Look, I only did what I needed to do," Kevin said with a scoff. "Preston made a ton of money, I needed help, he refused, so I sued him. I won," he shrugged mildly. "I had nothing to feel guilty about. We had an agreement, and he screwed me over. But of course Preston didn't see it that way."

"So, you thought you'd get rid of the problem altogether," Mitchell suggested in a smug tone. "That way Preston would never stand a chance of getting the money back."

"No," Kevin said firmly. "He never would have got the money back. He knew that. He exhausted all of his legal options. I won everything."

"You took everything from your brother?" Mitchell asked and studied the man before him intently. "You didn't see anything wrong with that?"

"No," Kevin growled. "All he had to do was share just a little. But he wouldn't. I helped him create his company, I helped him get the connections he needed to get the book marketed, I did all of the grunt work. I even helped him with some of the scenes in the books and as soon as he made it big he tried to forget he knew me. Some brother, right?"

"Not as bad as getting into a heated argument, then killing him," Mitchell countered and stood up from his chair abruptly. "Then you posed him like the victim from his book, was that one of the scenes that you helped him with?"

"Well, I, uh," Kevin stared up at Mitchell. "I didn't kill him," he insisted. "We did argue but I didn't kill him. Once I had spoken to him I realized that he had no intention of reconciling, so I left to fly home, but like I said they wouldn't let me on the plane."

"So, while you are supposedly sleeping at the airport, your brother was being murdered, by a hit man you didn't hire, and enacted like a scene in a book that you helped your brother write?"

Kevin ran his hands across his face and groaned through his splayed fingers.

"I didn't help him with his last book. I know it looks bad, but it's the truth. I wouldn't kill my brother, he's got kids, a wife, no matter how much I hated him, I wouldn't kill him!" Kevin cried out as he lowered his hands and looked up at Mitchell pleadingly.

"No, you would just hire someone else to do it for you," Mitchell barked out.

"I didn't, I didn't," Kevin cried out again. He started to tremble. "Please, can I have one smoke? Please?"

Mitchell rolled his eyes and looked up at the two-way mirror. Vicky could tell from his expression that he didn't think he was going to get any further with the questioning. Vicky's cell phone began ringing. She pulled it out to see it was Aunt Ida calling her.

"Hello?" she said as Mitchell began asking Kevin the same questions again.

"Vicky, I have an idea," Ida said. "In the book the person who hired the killer purchased one of those throw away cell phones at a shop to call him on," Ida explained. "Maybe whoever committed this crime did the same thing."

"Well, everything else has been by the book so far," Vicky agreed. "Maybe if we can get an eyewitness to the purchase of the phone, we will be able to prove it was Kevin."

"I'll head into town and check things out," Ida said swiftly.

"By yourself?" Vicky frowned hesitantly. "I don't know if that's such a good idea. If Kevin isn't the killer then the killer might try to do anything to stop us from searching."

"Don't worry, I'll have Rex with me," Ida assured her.

Chapter Eight

Vicky was still a little worried but she was glad to have the chance to check out something else she was suspicious about. The door to the room she was in swung open and Mitchell stepped inside. He closed it behind him.

"What are you doing in here?" he asked tensely.

"Sheriff McDonnell invited me to observe," Vicky replied hesitantly.

"Wow, he never fails to surprise me," Mitchell said as he shook his head.

"I'm sorry, I would have let you know, but you were in the middle of questioning Kevin," Vicky added.

"It's fine," Mitchell nodded and glanced towards the mirror where he could see Kevin sitting and shaking his head. "What did you think?"

"I think it's just as confusing as the rest of this case," Vicky admitted with a sigh.

"Sheriff McDonnell is desperate to solve this case. Especially considering the media firestorm that is going to blow up once the press gets wind of the way Preston was killed."

"Do you think Kevin did it?" Vicky asked as she looked into Mitchell's eyes.

"I don't know who else it could have been," Mitchell frowned. "There was some bad blood between the brothers, so it makes sense, but..." he paused.

"But you don't feel it?" Vicky supplied for him.

"He just looked so stunned when I told him his brother was dead. I wasn't expecting that," Mitchell admitted. "Either he's a great actor, or somehow he wasn't expecting the news. I'm going to give him a little break, and then I'll go at him again," Mitchell added.

"Do you know how Preston got into the restaurant after closing?" Vicky asked.

"No, none of the staff admitted to knowing anything about it," Mitchell said. "Maybe someone forgot to lock the door."

"Maybe," Vicky said quietly. But she specifically remembered reminding the staff to make sure they locked everything up. Why had the door been left unlocked?

"I'm going to head back to the inn," Vicky said. She wanted to talk to the staff and see if she could find out any more information.

Vicky drove Ida's car back to the inn. As soon as she arrived she headed for the staff lounge. When she stepped inside she noticed one of the young women from the kitchen staff sitting nervously at a large, round, wooden table.

"Hi Sherrie," Vicky said casually as she sat down at the table beside her.

"You know don't you?" Sherrie gasped out with tears already forming in her eyes. "Oh, Vicky, please don't fire me, I had no idea I swear!"

"Slow down, Sherrie," Vicky said sternly and looked into her eyes. She was barely older than eighteen and was training under Chef Henry. "Start from the beginning and tell me what happened."

"I know that the restaurant bar is supposed to be shut down at midnight," Sherrie admitted in a whisper. "But Preston caught me in the hallway. I knew who he was, because I'm a fan of his books. He begged me to leave the door unlocked to the bar. He said he'd had a rough day, that he just needed a quiet place where he could unwind. I knew it was against the rules, but I didn't think it would be a big deal. I guess," she paused a moment and lowered her eyes. "I guess I was just a little star struck. Maybe if I hadn't let him in, none of this would have happened," she wept and wiped at her eyes.

"Sherrie, you shouldn't have done that," Vicky sighed as she sat back in her chair. "But, this is not your fault. Someone was hired to kill Preston. If it hadn't been in the bar, I'm sure it would have been somewhere else," Vicky spoke with certainty but in the back of her mind she wondered if it would have. The killer wanted the crime to unfold in a very specific way. What if the bar had been unavailable? Would that have prevented Preston's death? But how convenient was it that Preston had pleaded with Sherrie to leave the door unlocked to the bar? Had someone invited him there? Was it part of the set-up?

Sherrie sniffled and nodded a little. It was clear she was still very shaken up. "I'm sorry, Vicky," she said mournfully.

"Mistakes happen," Vicky said softly. "We have our rules for a reason, Sherrie. But if you had called me and asked if you could let him in, I might have said yes," Vicky shrugged slightly. "We do our best to give our guests what they ask for."

"So, you're not going to fire me?" Sherrie asked hopefully.

"No, I'm not," Vicky replied. "But I do want to ask you something. Did you see a man that looked very similar to Preston anywhere near the bar, or the inn around the time you let Preston in? Was anyone else with Preston, or did he say he was meeting someone?"

"I didn't see anybody then," Sherrie shook her head. "But I saw someone that looked very similar to Preston before that. I saw Preston arguing with him. I noticed because I thought they looked so similar, they could be brothers."

"Did you hear anything they said?" Vicky asked hopefully.

"Uh," Sherrie closed her eyes for a moment. "Preston was saying, you've taken everything from me, you've taken everything. Now you're going to know how that feels."

"Are you sure it was Preston that said that?" Vicky asked with a furrowed brow.

"Yes, I'm sure," Sherrie nodded. "He said, now you're going to pay."

"You said the brothers looked similar, is there any chance you got them confused?" Vicky asked.

"No, because the other one was smoking," Sherrie said. "I remember, because I don't like the smell. I would have noticed if Preston smoked. So, when he said he had a rough day, I remembered the argument. I figured he just needed to blow off some steam."

Vicky was mystified by the revelation. If Preston had been threatening Kevin, would that be enough reason for Kevin to turn around and plan his brother's murder? Why would Preston invite his brother to the book launch just to threaten him? It all didn't seem to add up.

"I'm sorry again, Vicky," Sherrie said shamefully.

"It's okay," Vicky promised her. "Just take the rest of the day off, okay?"

"Thanks," Sherrie nodded as she sniffled.

As Vicky was leaving the room she was trying to piece things together. Her cell phone began to ring. She saw that it was Mitchell.

"Hey, I've got some interesting information," he said.

"So do I," Vicky replied. "You go first."

"Turns out our superstar author was flat broke," Mitchell explained quickly. "That lawsuit between himself and his brother wiped him out completely."

"But he was just about to launch the new book..." Vicky reminded him.

"But the book was not doing well at all," Mitchell continued. "His family's house is in foreclosure, the kids switched from private to public school due to non-payment of tuition, and the cars were about to be repossessed. He had less than nothing, he owed over a hundred thousand dollars."

"Wow," Vicky said with surprise. "Well, then what I just learned makes a little more sense."

"What's that?" Mitchell asked.

"One of the employees overheard Preston and Kevin fighting. She said that Preston told Kevin that he had ruined him, that he had taken everything from him, and that now Kevin was going to know what that was like," her voice trailed off as she processed the new information.

"But if that's true, if Kevin won everything from his brother, if he had already taken everything he could, why would he risk murdering him, too? It doesn't make any sense," Mitchell groaned with frustration.

"Wait," Vicky said quickly. "Think about it. If Preston, the author of the book, died the same way as the character in the book, it would create a huge amount of publicity for his new book. Maybe Kevin wanted to squeeze out every dime he could from his brother, even if it meant killing him in the process."

"That's a good thought," Mitchell agreed with admiration in his voice. "But the only problem is, this book was Preston's. Kevin had no stake in it. It was agreed in the lawsuit that Preston would keep all of the proceeds. Even now, any money the book sales draw in will go to Preston's widow."

"How odd," Vicky frowned. "And Kevin knew this?"

"Yes," Mitchell said. "It was all clearly detailed in the lawsuit."

"Maybe Kevin planned to sue anyway," Vicky suggested. "Or perhaps he would have inherited the money in the event of Preston's death?" Vicky suggested.

"I can check on that, but I doubt Preston would still consider Kevin family," Mitchell pointed out.

"Maybe not, but maybe he didn't have time to change things legally, and Kevin swooped in to kill him before he could make that change," Vicky frowned. She knew she was grasping at straws but she couldn't think of anything else that made sense.

"I'm going to check into that, and speak to Lyle again," Mitchell said

"Do you think I can sit in on the interrogation again?" Vicky asked hopefully.

"Might as well try while Sheriff McDonnell's in an accommodating mood," Mitchell suggested.

When Vicky hung up her phone and began walking back out of the lobby it suddenly hit her how tired she was. She had been running back and forth from the police station and couldn't even remember the last time she ate. She frowned as she wondered what would happen if the murder couldn't be solved. If Sheriff McDonnell was willing to offer a day off if it was solved, what was he going to do to Mitchell if it wasn't?

She decided she'd stop along the way and pick up a dozen donuts. Something to keep Sheriff McDonnell in his good mood. As she rolled through the drive through of the shop, she heard two of the employees talking through the half-open window.

"All I'm saying is if I lost everything, I don't know if I could keep going," one of the women was saying.

"You shouldn't even talk like that," the other woman warned her as she bagged up the donuts that Vicky had ordered. "There's always a reason to keep going."

"I don't know," the first woman argued. "If I knew that I could help my family more, by not being here anymore, I'd probably think about it at least. Wouldn't you?"

"Stop talking so morbid," the woman bagging the donuts complained. "Everything will work out. You know you're due for a raise, and I'm sure your parents will help out."

"It was just a hypothetical, Donna, no need to get so worked up," the first woman rolled her eyes.

"Here you go," she said to Vicky as she opened the window and handed her the donuts. Neither woman had any idea that Vicky had been listening to their conversation. But what they thought was a private discussion had sparked in Vicky's mind the beginning of an idea she could not bring herself to believe.

On the drive to the police station she began to piece everything together in her mind as she devoured a few donuts. She dropped the remaining donuts by Sheriff McDonnell's office, and he gave her permission to watch Mitchell at work.

Vicky watched through the two-way mirror as Mitchell's intimidating presence seemed to fill the interrogation room. It was impossible for her not to notice how handsome he looked. She tried to ignore how distracting she found him, but it was difficult.

"All right, Lyle, I need some answers," Mitchell said as he slapped a picture of Kevin down on the table in front of Lyle. "Is this the man who paid you for the murder?"

"Sure," Lyle shrugged mildly. "It looks like him."

"It looks like him, but is it him?" Mitchell growled sternly.

"I don't know man, how can I tell?" Lyle said with annoyance.

"Look closer," Mitchell commanded him as he picked up the picture and pushed it closer to the man's face. "Does this look exactly like the man who hired you? Keep in mind that we look favorably on any information you can provide us about the person that paid you to kill Preston."

"Hey, hold on a minute," Lyle snapped. "I did what I was paid to do. It's not like I take a picture of my clients. It's meant to be anonymous."

Mitchell sighed and adjusted his hat. As he did, he caught a whiff of his own cologne.

"Wait," Mitchell said as he leaned down closer to Lyle. "How did he smell? The man who hired you?"

"Smell?" Lyle narrowed his eyes. "You think I'm some kind of freak going around sniffing people?"

Mitchell slammed the photograph along with his fist down hard against the table. The sound was sharp enough that it even made Vicky jump. "Answer the question," Mitchell demanded as he glared into Lyle's eyes, his eyes flashing with warning.

"I guess, he smelled fine," Lyle stammered out. "I mean, he didn't smell like anything, that I noticed. He didn't stink or anything."

"What about cigarettes?" Mitchell pressed. "Did you smell any smoke on him?"

"No," Lyle shook his head. "And I would have noticed. That is such a nasty, dirty habit," he scrunched up his nose.

"Really?" Mitchell asked with a raised eyebrow.

"What?" Lyle asked innocently.

"You kill people for a living, but you think smoking is a terrible habit?" Mitchell questioned.

"I do my job," Lyle growled. "But I would never poison my body like that."

"Good to know," Mitchell flicked his eyes towards the mirror.

Vicky was already dialing Aunt Ida on her cell phone. She wanted to find out for certain if her suspicions were correct.

"Hello?" Ida answered breathlessly.

"Aunt Ida, are you okay?" Vicky asked as she heard a roar in the background.

"Yes sorry, I'm on Rex's bike," Ida explained quickly.

"Did you talk to the shop owners?" Vicky asked.

"I did, they said a man who looked like Kevin was in the shop, but I don't think it could have been Kevin," Ida said smugly.

"Why?" Vicky asked.

"Because I asked if he smelled like cigarette smoke, and the clerk who sold him the cell phone said he didn't. In fact he complained about one of the employees that was outside on a smoke break, said it was unprofessional."

"Thanks, Aunt Ida!" Vicky said as Mitchell stepped into the room with her. She hung up the phone and looked into Mitchell's eyes. He still looked a little riled up from the encounter with Lyle. "Aunt Ida says the clerk at the shop where the cell phone was purchased by one of the brothers, didn't think the buyer was a smoker, and they did say he looked like Preston."

"Ida needs to stop investigating on her own. But that's what Lyle said about the person that hired him," Mitchell sighed and pulled off his hat. He ran his hand back through his sandy brown hair. "He said he didn't smell of cigarette smoke, but he looked like Kevin and there's only one person that looks that much like Kevin."

"Preston," Vicky supplied.

"But how could that be possible? Why would Preston arrange his own death?" Mitchell sighed and rubbed at his eyes.

"Did you find out who would inherit the funds from the book becoming a bestseller?" Vicky asked quietly as she stood in front of him.

"Sure, just the usual, his wife and in the event of her passing, his children," Mitchell explained. "But the wife has an alibi, I checked it out. She was with one of the kids at the hospital. Apparently he broke his ankle. The nurse remembered her because she was arguing and crying over her bill," he added with a grimace.

Vicky leaned back against the stone wall of the interrogation room. She closed her eyes briefly as emotions washed over her before she opened them again to look at Mitchell once more.

"What is it?" Mitchell asked as he noticed the sorrow in her gaze. "What's wrong, Vicky?" he stepped closer to her.

"I don't think we're going to solve this murder," Vicky said quietly.

"Oh, don't give up on me, now," Mitchell pleaded as he took her hand in his.

"No, I would never give up on you, Mitchell," Vicky promised him and shook her head. "That's not what I mean. I mean I don't think we're going to solve this murder, because I don't think it ever was a murder, at least, not exactly."

"I think a bullet to the back of the head says differently," Mitchell pointed out with widened eyes.

"Maybe Preston didn't pull the trigger," Vicky frowned. "But I think that when he walked into the restaurant that night, he knew it would be his last."

"Why would you say that?" Mitchell asked, his curiosity growing.

"Think about it," Vicky said gently. "Preston had lost everything. His own brother had turned against him. His new book which he had pinned all of his hopes on was a disaster. He had to face the fact that he wasn't a great writer, not without his brother's help. So, as he processed all of this, he was angry, and he was desperate."

"I'm following you," Mitchell nodded slowly.

"He knew that he was washed up, a has been," Vicky pointed out. "He was losing his house, his cars, his family's respect. Maybe his wife calling about the broken ankle was the last straw, or maybe it just added to the pile."

"So, his only way to help them and to get his revenge on his brother was to stage his own death," Mitchell whispered. "How sad."

"It is sad," Vicky sighed. "He set everything up, pretended to be his brother, even brought Kevin here.

He probably changed Kevin's ticket so he couldn't fly out. With how similar they looked, he could have gotten away with just about anything. He wanted to make sure his family was okay financially knowing that the publicity from the murder would probably sell more books and he probably had a life insurance policy. He also wanted his brother to lose everything, just like he had. He wanted him to understand what it was like."

"Wow," Mitchell shook his head as he rested a hand on Vicky's shoulder. "I don't even know what to think about that."

"I think he thought it was a loving gesture," Vicky murmured sadly. "Too bad he didn't think about how devastated his family would be over all of this. I'm sure his children would have happily traded a private school education to have their father back."

"I'm sure," Mitchell agreed and pulled her gently into his arms. "I don't know how you figured this all out, Vicky, but you are brilliant."

"Murder is never brilliant, remember Mitchell?" she whispered beside his ear before resting her head on his shoulder. She closed her eyes and hugged him a little tighter. "Money isn't everything," she added.

"I know," he kissed her forehead softly. "Neither is a battle of wills. All that really matters is the time we have with each other."

"How do you think Kevin is going to take it?" Vicky asked softly.

"I honestly don't know," Mitchell frowned. "Despite what he did to his brother, I don't think he was expecting any of this. But I guess it's time to let him know the truth."

Vicky stared at the empty interrogation room wondering how Kevin was going to take the news. She watched with bated breath as Mitchell walked with Kevin into the interrogation room. He sat down across from Kevin calmly. Kevin looked at him warily.

"You can threaten me all you want," Kevin said sternly. "But I didn't kill my brother."

"No, you didn't," Mitchell agreed with a heavy sigh.

"I didn't hire anyone to do it either," Kevin added with a glare.

"I know you didn't," Mitchell agreed.

Kevin looked at him strangely. "What are you saying? Did you find out who did this?" he demanded.

"Kevin, maybe you didn't pull the trigger, maybe you didn't pay for the hit, but what did you think was going to happen when you pulled everything out from under your brother?" Mitchell asked as he studied the man who looked so similar to the person who had been carted off to the morgue.

"I don't know. I just wanted him to realize what he did was wrong," Kevin muttered and shook his head. "Why does this matter? Who killed my brother?" Kevin demanded.

Mitchell cleared his throat. "Kevin, it looks like Preston planned all of this himself."

"That's ridiculous," Kevin sputtered out. "Why would he do something as crazy as that?"

"Maybe because he felt like he had nothing left to lose?" Mitchell suggested.

"Are you saying he tried to frame me for his murder?" Kevin asked, his eyes wide.

"It would have worked, too," Mitchell said sternly. "All the evidence pointed to you. He did an excellent job of setting you up. Except, he forgot one very important thing."

"What?" Kevin asked with disbelief.

"You're a smoker," Mitchell pointed out. "Even though he was pretending to be you, he didn't think of or couldn't bring himself to embrace the habit."

"He hated cigarettes," Kevin muttered under his breath. "He always said they'd kill me. Who could have imagined that they would be what proved my innocence?"

"Well, you're free to go," Mitchell said quietly. "We'll have some follow up questions and paperwork for you."

"What am I supposed to do now?" Kevin asked with disbelief. "How am I supposed to face his wife and kids?"

"What you do with your life now is your choice," Mitchell shrugged. "But I think Preston's actions have taught us all a few things."

"Yes, yes they have," Kevin nodded as he stood up from the table. Mitchell opened the door for Kevin, and glanced over at the two-way mirror where he knew Vicky was still watching, before he stepped out after him. Vicky smiled faintly, as if she thought Mitchell could see her. She knew that he was exhausted, that the case had put him through the wringer, but she could see the gratitude in his eyes when he looked in her direction. She felt the same gratitude for him. No matter the difficulty they were facing, they were always grateful to have each other.

Chapter Nine

Slowly but surely Mitchell was able to confirm everything Vicky had said. Preston's wife had found a note he left for her that explained everything as well. She hadn't found it right away because of being in the hospital with her son. As the media got wind of the story, they didn't care that it had all been a set-up, that just made it all the sweeter for them. There was even talk of a movie deal in the works.

Even though Vicky hadn't known Preston or his family personally, something about his case made her bewildered. It was hard to think of someone taking their own life for the sake of revenge. Preston's family would be well taken care of, and Kevin would walk free. Lyle would receive his full sentence since he couldn't arrange a plea bargain as the person who hired him was the person he killed. He would be off the streets for the rest of his life.

Sarah was able to get the inn straightened out after the chaos, and everything felt as if it was getting back to normal. But Vicky just couldn't shake the uneasy feeling in the pit of her stomach. Perhaps it was because of Preston choosing the inn to stage his own murder. He could have done it anywhere, but ended up at the inn. With a crime so planned out and detailed she had to wonder if just one thing had gone wrong, would he have called it off.

"I'm leaving," Ida said as she hugged Vicky, pulling her out of her thoughts. "Are you sure you're going to be okay?" she asked as she looked into her niece's eyes.

"Sure," Vicky managed a smile. "You are way overdue for some fun, Aunt Ida."

Ida looked phenomenal, adorned in black leather with a hot pink motorcycle helmet tucked under her arm. She stared at her niece for a long moment.

"But don't you realize, sweetheart, so are you?" Ida asked and then leaned over to kiss her cheek. "Don't let these moments pass you by, sweetheart."

Vicky was a little startled by her aunt's words, but they hit home. As she watched her aunt climb onto the back of her motorcycle and head off down the road with Rex she felt a slight urge to follow her, to experience some of that freedom. But she felt a stronger urge to call Mitchell. She had barely seen him since the crime had been solved. Sheriff

McDonnell went on a tirade about the amount of paperwork that had to be done and the in-depth research it was going to take to prove that Preston's death was indeed paid for by himself. Mitchell of course, was doing his best to meet all of his boss' demands. Since Vicky had nothing else to do she had insisted that Sarah take the weekend off to be with her family. But with the inn finally quiet, there really wasn't much to do.

Vicky walked around the side of the inn, her mind still lingering on Mitchell. When she stepped out into the garden her nerves were soothed by the sight of the beautiful blossoms surrounding her. She wanted a few moments alone with the sunset to find some peace. When she heard footsteps slowly approaching from behind her she grew nervous.

Could they have been wrong about the murder all along? Was there still a killer roaming free? Her heart was in her throat when she turned swiftly to confront what she expected to be an attacker. She nearly buried her face in a bouquet of red roses.

"Oops," Mitchell muttered as he drew the flowers back before her face could strike them. "Are you okay,

Vicky?" he asked with concern as he looked into her eyes.

"Yes, sorry, just surprised," Vicky laughed at her own reaction. "Are those for me?" she asked with a small, sweet smile.

"Yes," he replied nervously and held them out with a trembling hand.

"Are you okay, Mitchell?" Vicky laughed as she took the roses and sniffed the blooms. "They are lovely," she sighed.

"I just wanted to see if I could steal a moment with you," he whispered as he stepped closer to her, his eyes shimmering in the shifting light of the sunset. "Do you mind?"

"I couldn't think of any better way to spend my time," Vicky smiled in return and kissed him softly on the lips. As much as she wanted to continue, she felt a little guilty. "But I know you must be tired, don't you want to be at home resting?"

He studied her intently, a distant emotion lingering in his gaze that Vicky couldn't quite place.

"There's only one place I ever feel rested," he murmured as he wrapped his arms loosely around her waist. "In your arms," he smiled and kissed her gently.

"Aw," Vicky grinned up at him and wrapped her arms around him, drawing him closer. "That's a place you can always count on," she promised as she nestled close to him.

"Always?" he asked as he drew a strand of her hair back away from her face so that he could continue to look deeply into her eyes. Vicky felt a little uncertain. He was so hard to read sometimes. She found herself wondering if he was upset or elated. She couldn't tell which.

"Of course always, Mitchell," she replied as she smiled faintly. "Don't you already know that?"

"I guess I just wanted to make sure," he murmured, still holding her gaze.

"Why?" Vicky frowned a little. "Have I done something to make you feel otherwise?"

"No, not at all," he replied with a hint of a smile. "I just thought it might be a good idea to double check."

"Okay," Vicky laughed and shook her head at him. "What's gotten into you tonight, Mitchell?"

"I just think, every day, life changes," Mitchell explained in a soft voice. "People are born, people die."

"Yes," Vicky agreed as she continued to study him quizzically.

"I just mean," Mitchell hesitated, his deep southern accent making his stammering even more endearing. "The things we think are promised to us, the things we think will always be there, those are the things that we tend to take for granted."

"Mitchell, I know you've been busy, and it's okay," Vicky assured him swiftly. "I understand how important your job is, and I know how brave you are to do it."

"But do you understand how important you are?" he asked and pulled back slightly from her embrace. He found her hands with his own and drew them against the warmth of his palms, his gaze still held to hers.

"Sure I do," Vicky replied with a nervous smile. "Really Mitchell, there's nothing to worry about, I'm here with you, always," she looked into his eyes, hoping that he believed her. It surprised her sometimes that she had such strong feelings for him. She had never felt this way about anyone and used to doubt that she ever would.

He smiled. "I'm glad you feel that way," he murmured, a flush rising in his cheeks. Vicky watched as he began to lower himself onto one knee. Her eyes widened and her heart began to race. She couldn't believe what she was seeing. She had no idea if she was ready for it, she had certainly not been expecting it, but whether she was ready or not he still pulled the ring box out of his pocket anyway. He held it open in front of him, offering it to her as he looked up at her. "Vicky, I want to spend the rest of my life with you, and I hope you feel the same. I don't want to waste a moment that I could be sharing with you. I don't want to think about the future anymore, I want our future to be now. Will you marry me?"

Vicky squeaked and placed her hand lightly against the base of her neck to try to cover the sound. She stared down at the ring sparkling in the last of the sunlight, then back up into the bluest eyes she had ever seen. Mitchell was waiting nervously for her answer, but all she could do was gaze at him lovingly.

"Vicky?" he asked hesitantly and shifted slightly on his knee. "It's okay if you say no."

"No?" Vicky asked with surprise, her eyes wide with shock.

"Okay," he nodded and closed the ring box, his cheeks flushing with embarrassment. "I was rushing things a little, I know," he grimaced.

"No! Not no! I didn't mean no!" Vicky gasped out and grasped his face gently between her palms. "I meant why would I ever say, no? Yes, Mitchell, a thousand times yes!" she smiled down at him. She never thought she would want to marry anyone but she couldn't imagine not being with Mitchell for the rest of her life.

In the same moment that he leaned up to kiss her, she leaned down to kiss him, and their lips collided earlier than expected. It knocked Mitchell slightly off balance, and as he tried to straighten himself, Vicky's weight pushed against him and they both tumbled down into the lush grass of the garden. Yet their kiss never broke. As they lay entangled in each others' arms with the ring box nestled in the grass beside them, the petals on the blooms in the garden rustled beneath the mildest wind, as if offering applause. The first stars of the evening began to dot the sky, and Vicky couldn't think of a single place she would rather be.

The End

More Cozy Mysteries by Cindy Bell

Heavenly Highland Inn Cozy Mystery Series

Murdering the Roses

Dead in the Daisies

Killing the Carnations

Drowning the Daffodils

Bekki the Beautician Cozy Mystery Series

Hairspray and Homicide

A Dyed Blonde and a Dead Body

Mascara and Murder

Pageant and Poison

Conditioner and a Corpse

Makeup, Mistletoe and Murder

Hairpin, Hair Dryer and Homicide

Blush, a Bride and Body

Shampoo and a Stiff

Made in United States
North Haven, CT
20 January 2024

47668041R00078